Lone Cypress

론 사이프러스

※ 한·영 시집 ※

론 사이프러스
Lone Cypress

이 병 호

지식공감

마치 손님이 이발소에 오면 이발사는 의자에 앉게 하고 손님이 어떻게 원하는지 물어본다. 손님이 원하는 대로 머리를 다듬고 깎고 마무리해서 손님이 좋아하면 그때야 입가에 미소가 스며든 것처럼 시인도 시상이 떠오르면 윤곽을 잡고 사고하고 생각한 것을 써내려 가다가 마음에 들지 않으면 다시 고쳐 쓰고 마무리해서 인고의 시간을 거친 다음 겨우 마음에 드는 시를 내놓을 수 있어서 밝은 미소를 지을 수 있다.

문학을 좋아해서 쓰지 않으면 안 될 것만 같은 사명감에 젖어 용기를 내어 조금씩 조금씩 써 모아서 조그마한 시집을 냈습니다. 시인뿐만 아니라 문학을 하는 사람들은 읽어줄 독자도 생각해서 독자가 좋아하고 읽히는 글을 써야 하는 책임감 내지는 의무감이 있다고 생각한다.

옛말에 호랑이는 죽어서 가죽을 남기고 사람은 이 세상을 떠나면서 이름을 남긴다고 했는데 글 쓰는 사람은 자연과 사회를 벗삼아 생활하면서 거기에서 우러러 나오는 사회상, 가치관, 인생관을 조명하고 포용하면서 문학을 통해서라도 사회의 정서를 순화하고 정화하는데 앞장서야 한다고 생각한다.

4

이번 첫 번째 시집을 내면서 앞으로 더욱더 정진하고 매진하여 잘 읽히고 좋은 시를 더 많이 생산하도록 하는 계기로 삼으려고 한다.

이번 시집을 내는 데 있어서 많은 도움을 주신 한국문인협회 미주지회장으로 수고하신 강정실 회장님께 심심한 사의를 표하는 바입니다.

- 2015년 5월
몬터레이에서 이병호

꽃잔디 해변

: 아날로그 시대

고향 동네 이발소
손님 없는 빈자리에 주인은 연신
파리채를 벽을 향해 탁탁 치고 있다

8월의 무더위는
숭숭 구멍이 난 부채를 얼굴에다 흔들어 보지만
이마에는 땀방울이 맺혀 있다

그래도 수박만한 희망을 품고
뜨거운 여름 한낮을 살갑게 찾아올
손님을 기다리며 연신 파리채와 부채를
가지고 논다

한때 문전성시를 이루던 때가 있었다
길게 자란 머리칼을 잘라내고
덥수룩한 흰 근심을 말끔히 다듬으며
가위 하나로 버틴 세월이다

금이 간 거울을 옆문을 빠져나오면
대추잎 무성한 우물가가 보이고
비누거품을 풀고 허공에 쓱쓱 문댄
낮달이 면도칼은 시퍼렇게 누워있다

이발소 벽에 걸려 있는
벽시계의 뻐꾸기가 뻐꾹 뻐꾹
비눗갑에 고인 적막을 한 번씩
휘젓고 돌아간다

속도를 섬기는 지금의 시대
아날로그는 둔하고 불편스럽다
그래도 그때의 정(情)이 그리워
8월 무더운 날에 적어 본다

: 정겨운 모습

어느 오후 한나절
따스한 햇볕 아래 공원 벤치에 앉아 시간 가는 줄 모르고
바닷가를 바라보면서 장미꽃을 피워가는 젊은 남녀가 정겹
습니다

노년의 부부가
손을 꽉 부여잡고 집주변 오솔길을 말없이 터벅터벅 걸어가는
못다 푼 세월의 모습이 정겹습니다

오색 단풍에 물들어 산들바람 마셔가며
낙엽을 밟고 언약의 팔짱을 낀 채
세상만사 뒤로하고 산사를 향하여 가는 중년 부부가 정겹
습니다

아침 일찍이 등 뒤에 책가방 메고
친구들과 꿈을 안고 밝은 미소로 학교로 향하여 가는
학동들이 정겹습니다

비 오는 날 우산을 받쳐 들고
목적지를 향하여 정답게 걸어가는
연인들의 미소가 정겹습니다

∶ 참새떼

뒷마당의 나뭇가지 사이에
참새떼가 재재거린다.

어제도
오늘도
내일도
타악기와 관악기 그리고
현악기의 합주가 요란하다

참새떼가 노래하면
내가 듣다가
그에 화답하는 뜻에서
내가 노래하면
화들짝 놀라 날아가 버린다

여러 사람과 함께
여러 동물과 함께
주고받고 싶은데
서로가 외래어라
이해하지 못하고 헤어진다

: 5월

햇살이 넘실대는
모래언덕에 올라
닫혔던 마음의
빗장을 풀어헤친다

밀물처럼 쏟아져 들어오는
봄바람의 따스함은
내 고향 진달래처럼
곱기도 하다.

퐁퐁퐁 솟아나는 그리움
뛰쳐 가고 싶은
까까머리 친구네 집
다들 무얼 하고 있을까

까닭없는 울렁거림은
먼 옛날
바람처럼 가버린 사춘기
고향의 5월은
이미 길을 잃고
내 안에 들어와
이렇게 파도치고 있다

∶ 봉숭아 꽃

장가가던 날
새색시 손톱에다
봉숭아 꽃 물들어 주었다

첫날밤에는
새색시 발톱에도
봉숭아 꽃 물들어 주었다

미국에 있는 집에도
아이들에게 손톱과 발톱에
봉숭아 꽃 물들어 주려고
앞마당에다 곱게 심었다

옹기종기 모여 앉아
봉숭아 꽃을 물들이며
옛이야기를 하려는데
다들 어디로 가고
헛물만 켜 먹는다

: 사과를 씹다

붉은 사과 한 알을
어금니로 깨문다
새콤달콤한 즙이
목을 타고 넘어간다
가슴이 아무리 넓어도
안기지 않는다

불꽃 같은 정열이
언제 살아 있기나 했었나
세월은 흘러 이빨로
씹는 어금니만 아프다

책상 위에 사과를 내려놓는다
그런데 컴퓨터에
찍혀있는 깨문 사과 한 알이
애태우다 검게 타버린
이파리 한 잎과 함께
덤불 속으로 추락한다

: 꽃잔디 해변

해동아
우울한 날에는
꽃잔디 해변에 가자

해변 가득
연분홍 물감 풀어놓은 듯
그늘마저 눈부신 꽃들판에
꽃잔디를 보러 가자

눈비와 바람이 맵찬
추운 겨울 다 잊고
너끈히 한세상 이룬
꽃잔디밭 속을 거닐다 보면
아픔도 환한 빛이 되리라

해동아
슬픈 날에는
봄 하늘과 연분홍이 정분 난
꽃잔디를 보러 가자

∷ 선인장 소묘

천년의 침묵은 비碑가 되는가
인고의 삶을 이고 온 역경의 역사
햇볕 따가운 열기에 합장하는가
새들은 주변을 돌아 줄기를 트고
삶의 보금자리를 찾는다

어느 누구도 건들지 말라고
가시로 방패 삼아
지나가는 세월에 그리움 안겨 보내고
매서운 비바람에도
굳건히 서 있는 너의 자태
고난도 역경도 하늘을 우러르며
깊은 뿌리를 생명선에 지탱한다

내일의 환한 미소를 위해
긴 호흡 하늘로 내뿜는다

: 석류

꽃이 핀 지 얼마나 되었을까
벌써 껍질을 박차고 세상에
얼굴을 내미는 새빨간 알들이
처녀의 부푼 젖가슴처럼
금방이라도 터져 나올 것 같다

조심스럽게 쪼개보면 조물주의 작품
조화와 균형이 넘실거린다
정연하게 빈틈없이 제자리에 앉아
미소를 머금고
때를 기다리나 보다
맛은 신선하고 새콤달콤한 것이
살며시 혀끝을 자극한다
지금도 늦지 않으니
인생의 멋과 맛을 선사하며
석류알 같아 보이리라
주는 것이 받는 것보다 복이 있나니

: 벌새

새 중에서 가장 작은 새
쏜살같이 꽃으로 날아와
정지 상태에서 빠른 속도로 날갯짓한다

순식간에 송곳 같은 부리로 꿀을 따 먹으며
이꽃 저꽃으로 옮겨 다닌다

피곤한가 보다 나뭇가지에 앉아서 휴식을 청한다.
어느덧 보고 싶은가 짝을 부른다

비가 오나 바람이 부나
꽃을 찾아다니며
꽃들의 향기에 취하지도 않고
새콤달콤한 꿀만 먹고 사는 새
조그마한 것이 비행속도는 화살과도 같은데
오늘도 쉬지 않고 꽃 여행을 다닌다

뒤뜰에 핀 장미

꽃봉오리가 세상에 나온 지 엊그제 같은데
어느덧 세월 따라 뒤뜰에 활짝 핀
새빨간 장미꽃 한 송이

스치는 바람결에 아름다운 미소가 넘친다
설레는 마음으로 넌지시 다가가니
말없이 뿜어내는 상긋한 향기 속에

사랑의 속삭임이 메아리친다
오랜만에 만난 연인들처럼

: 난(蘭)

세상의 온갖 풍파에서 벗어나
한 송이의 꽃망울을 터트리기 위해
얼마나 인고의 시간이 흘렀는가

인내를 무기 삼아 실망과 허탈을 겪으면서
살며시 적막을 뚫고
어느 날 꿈을 펼치기 위해 피어오른다

순수함과 아름다움을 뿜어내고
모나리자의 미소를 품어내며
정숙한 여인의 마음을 설레게 하네

오랜 침묵 속에 변함없는 고아한 자태
한 점 부끄럼 없이 화려함을 자랑하고
탐욕과 혼란의 세상에서
기다림을 먹고사는 꽃

모르는 사이 꽃잎이 떨어지면
가난한 마음에 사랑이 채워지도록
돌아올 님을 기다리려나 봐

낙엽(Fallen leaves)

봄이 오면
깊은 잠에서 깨어 세상에 새 얼굴을 내밀고

여름이 오면
보이지 않는 호흡으로 생명을 나누어주면서
파릇파릇한 삶을 즐긴다

가을이 오면
형형색색으로 즐거움을 선사하다가
어느덧 바람결에 지상에 낙하하면
색이 바랜 잎사귀 밟는 소리에 세월을 깬다

겨울이 오면
소리도 없이 벌거숭이 되어
세상사를 경험하다가
또 다시 긴잠을 청한다

2부

캐나다 기러기

: 시간

시간은 간다
공간을 초월하여
시작도 없이 끝도 없이
어제를 뒤로하고
오늘도 가고 내일도 간다

시간은 간다
말도 없이 소리도 없이

시간은 간다
짜증도 없이 불평도 없이

시간은 간다
멈추지도 않고 쉬지도 않고
골짜기에서 물이 흘러 강으로
바다로 가듯이

시간은 간다
막을 수도 없고
붙잡을 수도 없이

시간은 간다
세상만사를 경험하고
희로애락을 보며

시간은 간다
당신도 모르게
나도 모르게
아무도 모르게

시간은 간다
지금도 영원히

: 일본군 위안부

하늘도 울고 땅도 울었다
태평양 전쟁 중에 아무 영문도 모른 채
꽃다운 나이에 강제로 일본군 위안부로 징용되어 가던 날
평생 씻지 못할 육신의 상처와 정신의 아픔을 안았다

부모 처자식도 없는가 일본군은
티끌만 한 양심의 가책도 없는가

인간의 위대성과 존엄성을 송두리째 짓밟았던 그날
천황(天皇)이 연합군에 항복했던 것처럼
대한한국 국민에 반성하고 사죄하라
다시 한 번 다짐해 본다

누가 뭐래도 한 맺힌 약소국가는 되지 말자
오늘도 역사의 수레바퀴는 돌아가는데
사실과 진실 앞에 역사 왜곡이 웬 말인가
매일매일 국력(國力)을 배양(培養)하자

조국(祖國)의 앞날을 위해
기나긴 겨울이 가면 봄이 오듯
어두운 밤이 지나면 태양은 다시 떠오른다

∶ 용기와 소신

라 브뤼에르는 재치 있게 지껄일 수 있는
위트도 없고,
그렇다고 해서
침묵을 지킬 만큼의 분별력도 가지지
못한다는 것은
커다란 불행이라고 말했습니다

나 또한 위트가 없고,
마냥 침묵을 지킬 자신도 없지만
아무렇지 않습니다
이유는 나름의 소신이 있기 때문입니다
세상은 재치 있는 사람을 선호한다지만
그렇지 못한 사람이 더 많습니다

대신 잘할 수 있는 나만의 특기가 있습니다
꼭 말해야 할 때
나는, 말할 수 있는 소신과
용기가 있으니 아무렇지 않습니다

: 행복을 찾는 길

딸이 물었습니다
아빠는 왜 항상 화내고 있어? 아빠 무슨 일 있어?
나는 매일매일 즐겁게 웃고 있었는데
딸의 말을 듣는 순간 깜짝 놀랐습니다
재미있게 웃고 있는 순간에도 인상을 쓰는가 싶었습니다

학교 화장실 거울을 보며 수시로 웃는 연습을 하는데
처음에는 영 어색했습니다
미간의 주름은 숟갈로 빡빡 밀고 코 주변에는 팔자 미소를
짓는 모습을 보이려고 많은 날을 연습했습니다
그 탓인지 요즈음은 아주 자연스러워졌습니다
이 기간까지 오랜 연습이 필요한 것 같았습니다

아내가 물었습니다
별로 좋은 일도 없는데 왜 웃고 있어요? 내가 그렇게
하찮게 보여요?
나는 진짜로 매일매일 즐거움 마음으로 웃고 있는데 아내의
말을 듣는 순간 뒤통수에 돌멩이를 맞은 기분이었습니다

그런데 말입니다. 요즈음 저를 보는 사람마다
무슨 즐거운 일이 있느냐? 무슨 안 좋은 일이 있느냐?
상반된 질문의 묻는 횟수가 늘어납니다
웃어야 할지, 울어야 할지 정말 모르겠습니다

그래도 행복은 찾는 웃음은 계속 찾아야 할 것 같습니다
어차피 한 번뿐인 인생인데 행복을 위해서는 이보다
못할 일이 어디에 있겠습니까

∶ 은혜(恩惠, Grace)

값없이 베풀어 주는 것
갚을 길이 없는 것
끝이 없는 것
기억에 남는 것
놀라운 것
시간과 공간을 초월하는 것
아름다운 것
하늘보다 높고 바다보다 넓은 것
한없이 사랑하는 것
후회가 없는 것

: 비(雨)

비가 내린다
강바닥 논바닥이 거북이 등처럼 금이 쩍쩍 갈라져
타들어 간 지도 오래되는데
금비가 내린다

가뭄이란 말이 무색할 정도로 사람들의
애간장을 태우더니
하늘도 사람들의 애절한 부르짖음을
들었는가

단비가 내린다
땅이 촉촉해지니 모든 것이 웃음을 머금고
새록새록 돋아난다

비야비야 쉬지 말고 내리거라
해갈하기에 충분할 정도로
농부들의 이마에 주름이 펴지도록
주룩주룩 내리거라

환한 미소는 여운을 남기고
올해도 마음은 벌써 풍년을 기약하는데
늦은 비가 소록소록 내린다

: 행복

거리마다 먹거리가 넘친다
먹거리 골목에는 여러 종류의 냄새가 코를 진동한다
TV와 컴퓨터를 열어도 먹는 게 차고 넘쳐난다
그래서일까 라디오, 신문에도 먹는 타령뿐이다
모든 게 다 차고 넘친다
그런데 어릴 때 빈곤을 견디며 성장했는데
더 많이 가진 지금이 행복하지 않다

행복은 풍요에 있는 것이 결코 아니다
모든 것에 감사한 마음을 가져야 행복해진다
불신보다는 조그만 일에도 감사한 마음을 느끼면
그게 행복인 것이다
행복해서 감사한 게 아니고
감사해서 행복한 것이 아닐까 싶다

: 고속도로를 달리며

달린다
속도제한을 염두에 두고
행선지를 향하여
앞차도 보고 뒤차도 보고 옆차도 보면서
인생도 달리고
마음도 달리고
시간도 달린다

가정과 직장과 사회를 그리며
과거도 달리고
현재도 달리고
미래도 달린다

하루하루가 고달파도
인내가 보약이 되도록
긴장과 스트레스를 풀면서
즐거운 마음으로 달린다

희망도 달리고
꿈도 달린다
행선지에 도착할 때까지
내일을 향하여
행복을 싣고서

: 소슬바람 부는 날

파란 융단 위
춤추는 갈매기 떼가 나르고
파도소리 합창단의 노랫소리
모두 떠나버린
허허로운 바닷가에서부터
소슬바람이 분다

어깨 아프도록 때리며 지나가는 바람
미친 듯 가슴을 헤집고 돌아다니는 바람
여기저기 피가 상흔(傷痕)을 남기며 달려가는 바람

실타래처럼 엉켜 놀던
바람난 소슬바람이 사고를 쳤다
모래언덕 위를 덮은
누더기마저 벗기고 혼자 간다
앙상한 내 주먹은 춥다고 운다
그림자를 길게 늘이면서 꺼이꺼이 홀로 운다

: 산고기탕 집

밖은 춥고 함박눈이 쏟아지는데
탕집 안은 손님과 열기로 북새통이다
어느 탁자 위엔 노루탕, 어느 탁자 위엔 토끼탕
어느 탁자 위엔 꿩탕이 노래를 합창한다

맥주 한잔으로 건배하고 회포를 풀며
추억의 역사를 만들어 간다
누가 한마디 한다 "사는 것이 그렇고 그런디
나더러 어쩌란 말이여"
거기엔 가정사도 있고 인생사도 있다

사는 것이 어렵고 힘들어도
반짝이는 별빛 속에 내 몸을 맡긴다
시간을 뚫고서 날고 싶은 새가 되고 싶다
돌아올 수 없는 올해도 며칠 안 남았는데
세월이 도망가기 전에 못다한 일 정리하고
내일을 새로운 꿈으로 단장하려다

: 캐나다 기러기

겨울이 되어 머나먼 수천 리 길을
산을 넘고 강을 건너 날아와 이곳까지 찾아왔네
일 년 내내 덥지도 않고 춥지도 않은
이곳에 삶을 찾아 기나긴 여정을
짝과 함께 올 때는 서로서로 돌아가기로 기약했는데
몇 해 전부터는 고향의 그리움을 잊어버리곤
어느덧 이곳 생활 환경에 익숙해졌나 봐
시간의 바퀴는 돌아가는데 변함없는 생활
어느 사람도 탓할 수가 없나 보다

풀밭에서 떼를 지어 짝을 이루고 풀을 뜯어 먹고
옆 호수에서는 한가롭게 헤엄을 치고
어느새 낳았는지 새끼들도 뒷뚱뒷뚱 걷는
엄마 뒤를 졸졸 따라다니네
걱정도 근심도 모른 체 하루하루가 여유만만한가 보네

부부애가 각별한가
누군가가 가까이 다가오면
감히 여기가 어디인 줄 알고 접근하려느냐는 표정으로
수컷은 긴 목을 곤두세우고 경고의 소리를 내고
머리를 두리번거리며 보초를 서는가 하면

암컷은 아랑곳없이 풀을 뜯다가 쉬기도 하고
낮잠을 청하기도 하면서
세월 가는 줄 모르고 평화로운 망중한을 보내며
내일의 운명은 알지도 못한 채
앞으로 가야 할 길은 멀고도 먼데
하루하루가 행복한 삶으로 잇대어지도록
가벼운 발걸음을 옮기려나 봐

∶ 나그넷길

한 발 한 발 지구를 밟는다
좁은 길 넓은 길을
날마다 생의 바퀴를 옮긴다

구부러진 길 곧은 길로
길의 끝은 보이지 않아도
한 가닥 소망을 품고
세상 풍파를 이겨가며
가야 할 길을 걸어가고

갈 길은 멀고 험해도
화평과 인내를 벗삼아
갈 길을 가야 하고

인생길을 걸으면
오르막이 있는가 하면 내리막도 있는데
괴로움과 어려움이 몰려와도
이 길을 걸어가야 하네
선택의 여지 없이
짧은 길도 먼 길도
가야 하고

곤하고 지쳐도
세상의 명예 권위 세월 속에 묻어 두고
마음의 등불 되어 생명으로 이어지는 님의 뜻을 따라
빛이 인도하는 대로
이 길을 묵묵히 걸어가야 하네

: 농촌 소묘

소를 이용해 쟁기로 밭을 갈며
도시로 보낸 자식들을 위해
밀짚모자를 쓴 채 이마에
두 줄기 땀을 뻘뻘 흘리는
농부가 그래도 좋습니다

풍년을 기약하며 허리를 굽혀
못줄 따라 흥겨운 가락 속에
모내기하는
촌부와 부녀자들이 그래도 좋습니다

밭일을 끝내고 머리에 수건을 쓴 채
허리 뒷짐에 양손으로 호미를 잡고
구부정구부정 저녁을 지으려
집으로 향하는 아낙네가 그래도 좋습니다

광주리에 새참을 담아 머리에 이고
한 손에 막걸리 주전자를 들고
논두렁 길을 종종걸음으로 걸어오는
부녀가 그래도 좋습니다

새들을 쫓아버리라는 소식을 듣고
허수아비를 세워놓고
따뜻한 햇살을 가슴에 담고
바람결에 스쳐 가는 세월이 그래도 좋습니다

누렇게 익어가는 벼가 인고의 고개를 숙인 채
황금벌판을 수놓으며
산들바람에 맞춰 부르는 풍년가가 그래도 좋습니다

론 사이프러스

: 반딧불이

밤마다
도깨비 방망이가
숲 속에서 춤춘다

달걀귀신과 몽땅귀신은
밤마다 숲 속에서
꼬리에 귀신불을 붙여
숲 속을 밤새도록
휘이휘이 춤춘다

눈을 떠도 감은 듯
감아도 눈 뜬 듯
핏빛 속에 빠져
뛰어봐도 그 자리에서
허우적거리고 있다

아내는 울고 있고
나의 가슴은 마르고
잃어버린 아들의 얼굴은
풀벌레 울음소리
반딧불이 되어
애간장 태운다

: 내가 살던 고향

앞산 뒷산
개울가와 뚝 길에도
노랑 꽃구름 내려와
움막을 치고
나비떼가 춤추듯
샛노란 향을 뿜고
온 동네 마을은
아카시아 꽃바람으로
두 팔 휘저어
콧구멍을 막아 버린다

어느새
노랑무처럼
속옷까지 향내에 젖게 한다

: 별이 빛나는 밤에

낮이 변하여 밤이 되고
밤하늘이 문을 열면
수많은 별빛이 함박눈처럼 쏟아진다
은하수를 보면서
지구의 한 지점에 서 있는 나도
서로 눈빛으로 무언의 인사를 나눈다
어디로 갈 바를 모르고 방황할 때
나그네의 좌표가 되는 북극성도 보인다
고요와 적막 속에
갑자기 별똥별 하나가 무서운 속도로 선을 긋는다
우리 인생 모두가 빈손으로 왔다가
빈손으로 가는데

우주를 가슴에 품고
이 세상 것 뒤로하고
푯대만 바라보고 한발 한발 걸으련다
세상에 있는 모든 것이
육신의 정욕과 안목의 정욕과 이생의 자랑이니
한 점 부끄러움 없이 사노라면
나의 마음은 어느덧 하늘나라에 와 있다
별이 빛나는 밤에

：기도

찾아 오시네
대화 나누자고
물으시네
믿음 있느냐고
회개하라 하시네
천국이 가까웠노라고
감사합니다
사랑합니다
빛과 소금이 되어
내 발에 등이요 내 길에 빛인
복음의 편지를 온누리에 전하리

주님 이름으로

: 몬트레이 바닷가에서

하늘이 문을 열고 바다가 입을 벌리며
밝은 햇살이 온 세상에 미소를 머금고
몇 조각구름은 바람결에 배를 탄다

멀리 보이는 산들은 하늘 아래 병풍을 치고
바닷새들은 갈 길을 향해 희망을 안는다
한 폭의 산수화에 흠뻑 빠져들면
고깃배들은 항구를 향해 만선의 노래 부르고
지난날의 추억은 한 편의 영화에 새록새록 감긴다

잔잔한 파도가 바위에 화를 내면
못다 푼 고뇌들이 산산이 부서지고
새하얀 물보라에 꿈을 실으며
시간 가는 줄 모르는 사이
바다는 내 마음을 아는가
인생의 수레바퀴는 계속 돌아가는데
과거를 모래 속에 묻어버린 거기에
소망의 내일이 기다린다는 것을.

: 바닷가

바닷물은
하얀 방울을 만들고는
잠시 하늘로 올리며
물방울 놀이하다
이내 조약돌을 굴리고 논다

차르르 또르르
누가 옆에 있지 않아도
혼자서 잘도 논다

갈매기는 자맥질로 따낸
따개비를 하늘 높이 올라
바위에 떨어뜨려
국물맛까지 입맛 다지며
쪽쪽 빨아 먹는다

새 대가리라는 누명은
아무렇지도 않은 듯
계속해서 따개비를 따서
입에 물고 하늘로 올라
바위에 떨어뜨리는 일을
되풀이하고 있다

: 바닷가 바위

새벽녘 안개구름은
는개처럼 쏟아져 내리고
바다는 끊임없이
흰 보석을 캐고 있다

멀리 보이는 수평선에
눈을 베어도
콧속을 파고드는
비릿한 바닷내음에 취해
밤별이 친구가 될 때까지
수평선만 바라보다가
섬 지킴이 신세가 되었다

: 파도와 바위

잔잔한 파도가 산들바람 미소에
살랑살랑 춤을 추며
밀려오고 밀려간다
성난 파도가 바위에 화를 뿜어내도
분을 품지 않고 하얀 인내의 물거품을 토해낸다

거친 세파를 어떻게 견뎌 왔던가
파도에 맞아 찢기고 할퀴고 부서져도
수만 년 동안 침묵으로 세월을 보낸다

얼굴은 이 모양 저 모양으로 변해도
시련과 아픔을 뒤로하고
오늘도 모든 사욕을 파도에 실어 보내고
순풍에 달리는 돛단배처럼
푸른 행복을 한아름 싣고서 달린다

ː 바닷가 오솔길 따라

태고의 흔적을 간직한 채
태평양 바닷가 기암절벽 옆으로
해안선을 따라 길이 놓여 있는데
사람들은 제각기 걷고 뛰며
자전거를 탄다
붉은 태양은 야망을 품고
또다시 떠오르며
몇 조각 뜬구름들은
돛단배 되어 유유히 항해한다

바닷물결이 바위에 거침없이
분노를 발하면
하얀 물보라가 합창으로 잠재우고
신선한 아침 공기는
심장을 건드리며
환한 미소가 창공을 난다

저 멀리 안개가 피어오르고
바닷바람은 말없이
옷깃을 스쳐간다
갈매기들은 아침부터
허기가 지는지
소리치며 창공을 날아다닌다

갈등과 혼란의 세상에서
길가에 서 있는 크고 작은 나무들은
가는 세월에 생명을 맡긴 채
사랑스러운 호흡을 즐긴다

오가는 사람마다 서로 인사로 반기며
가는 길과 목적지가 달라도 가야 할 길은
반드시 가야 한다
갈 길이 멀고 험해도
희망의 가슴으로 나그네의 길을
오늘도 쉼 없이 걷는다

： 산(山)

뭉게구름이 나그네 되어 쉬었다 가는 쉼터
수만 년을 침묵으로 그 자리에 서 있는데
낮에는 태양 밤에는 별들과 속삭인다

비바람과 폭설에 매섭게 시달려도
가벼운 미소로 용서하누나

그래도 낙심과 절망은
어머님의 마음으로 승화시키고
희망과 용기가 불타오르네

인간의 도전은 받아들여도
인간의 한계를 시험하는데

수많은 세월이 흘러도 변함이 없어
가까이 있으나 멀리 있으나
거기에 네가 있어 인내를 벗 삼아
네 곁에 오른다

세월의 수레바퀴 속에서
세상만사 요동치는데
너는 어이 말이 없구나
산아, 산아 말해다오
오늘도 너를 향해 눈을 들리라

：론 사이프러스

타고난 운명인가 보다
한 번도 땅 위에 발을 내딛지 못하고
온갖 세월의 풍상을 이겨내고
태평양과 맞닿은 기암절벽 위에
홀로 외로이 뿌리를 내리고 서 있는 너

바닷바람과 안개를 벗 삼아
소나타를 뿜어내고
거친 파도소리에 선잠을 깨며
가는 시간에 못다 푼 꿈일랑 맡겨 버리고
찾아오는 손님들을 상냥한 미소로 반기는 너

한 폭의 현실 속에서
나는 이렇게 사노라고
무언의 독백을 쏟아내면
행복은 거기 가까이 있는 거라고 화답을 하면서
오늘도 후회 없는 하루를 보내려는 너

4부

우리 부부

: 글밭

오늘도 나는 너와 씨름한다

주먹을 불끈 쥐고
가슴을 치며
머릴 쥐어뜯으며
글밭에 달려가 봐도
진척은 별로 없고
커피잔에 자꾸 손이 간다

아무리 너를 이기려고 해도
승부가 나지 않는다
이렇게 너를 이기려 하고
너를 넘어뜨리려고 해도
나의 머리에서는 쥐부터 난다

높은 하늘과 옛 고향은
삼삼하게 눈에 들어오는데
아득한 옛날은 자꾸
나를 서글프게 만들어
미래의 공간을
쉼 없이 달리는 길을
차단하고 있다

하지만 글밭인 네가 있어
펼쳐놓은 여러 종류의 채소가
꽃 피고 열매 맺을 때
흘렸던 눈물
그 감동의 늪이 있어 좋다

오늘도
글밭에 간다
땅 깊숙이 삽질하고
물 뿌리고 수확한
열매를 가지고
백 리는 뛸 수 있을 터인데……

: 고희

고희(古稀)가
눈앞에 와 있다

오늘은 십이월 삼십일일
해마다 찾아오는 날이지만
오늘은 유난스레 눈물이 난다

머릿속에는
아직도 어릴 적 엄마의 얼굴이
스멀스멀 출렁이는 기억으로
향기로운 내음으로 펴져 있는데

늦은 귀갓길인데도
동네 몇 바퀴 돌아온 것밖에 없는데
코앞에 고희가
빙그레 웃고 있다

: 은퇴

대학에서 강산도 3번 반 변하게
가르치다가 때가 되어 손 떼다
그동안 받은 스트레스와 긴장도
눈 녹듯 녹아가고

시간은 화살처럼 너무 빨리 날아가는데
괴로움도 어려움도 산들바람에 실어 보내고
새로운 제2의 인생을 설계해 본다

그 세월에 희로애락도 많았는데
가르치는 즐거움 속에서 나도 모르게
머리가 희끗희끗해졌나 보다

양어깨에 건강과 소망을 메고 터벅터벅 걸으며
걸어온 길 뒤돌아 보지 않고 앞을 향하여
인내는 쓰지만, 그 열매는 단것처럼

ː 오해

오해는 하기 마련인데
생각이 달라서인가
이해의 폭이 작아서인가

오해는 있기 마련인데
시간이 달라서인가
사정이 달라서인가

오해는 오래가기 마련인데
감정의 양이 달라서인가
뜻을 알지 못해서인가
오해는 하기 마련인데
한세상 살면서 미워도 서로 풀고
싫어도 밝은 미소로 살아가시구려

∷ 돈이 뭐길래

돈이 뭐길래
돈 때문에 결혼하고 돈 때문에 남남이 된다
돈이 뭐길래
부부가 헤어지고 재혼도 한다
돈이 뭐길래
부모와 자식 간에 갈등이 생기고
형제간이 소원해진다
돈이 뭐길래
돈 때문에 살고 돈 때문에 죽는다
돈이 뭐길래
돈 때문에 성공하고 돈 때문에 실패한다
돈이 뭐길래

돈 때문에 사랑하고 돈 때문에 미워한다
돈이 뭐길래
돈 때문에 병이 낫고 병이 든다
돈이 뭐길래
돈 때문에 울고 웃는다
돈이 뭐길래 돈 때문에 부하게 살고 가난하게 산다
돈을 사랑함이 일만 악의 뿌리가 되나니
알맞게 벌어 분수에 맞게 살으시구려

: 바라는 것들

고독과 외로움이 있는 곳에
대화가 있기를
갈등과 오해가 있는 곳에
이해가 있기를
거짓과 왜곡이 있는 곳에
진실이 있기를 바라며 살아갑니다.

싸움과 다툼이 있는 곳에
화해가 있기를
암흑과 어둠이 있는 곳에
광명이 있기를 바라며 살아갑니다.

실수와 잘못이 있는 곳에
용서가 있기를
미움과 질투가 있는 곳에
사랑이 있기를 바라며 살아갑니다.

가난과 굶주림이 있는 곳에
구제가 있기를
전쟁과 테러가 있는 곳에
평화가 있기를
수고와 땀이 있는 곳에
기쁨과 행복이 있기를 바라며 살아갑니다

그렇게 살으시구려

언제 어디서 태어난 건 아예 묻지 말고
불평과 불만이 있어도 그렇게 살으시구려

괴로움과 어려움이 있어도 한숨 쉬지 말고
짜증나고 화가 나도 그렇게 살으시구려

장래가 불투명하고 불확실해도 낙심하지 말고
근심과 걱정이 있어도 그렇게 살으시구려

남의 탓하지 말고 남의 일 간섭하지 말고
하는 일에 감사하며 그렇게 살으시구려

나 사는 것 다른 사람과 비교하지 말고
인생은 짧아도 아름다우니 그렇게 살으시구려

믿음 소망 사랑 끝까지 버리지 말고
앞길 열어주시는 주님만 믿고 그렇게 살으시구려

: 우리 부부

세상에 태어나 많고 많은 사람 중에서 부부가 된다는 사실에
우리 부부는 사람을 아래위로 은밀히 훑어본다는 맞선이란
걸 보았고
두 달을 넘기기 지루해 인생의 새 출발을 알리는 종소리를
울렸는데
부부란 인연으로 어언 사십여 년이란 세월을 화살처럼 날아
갔네요

아메리칸 드림이라는 가슴 설레는 언어에 포로가 되어
새 땅을 밟아도 중력을 느끼지 못했던 시절도 있었고
티격태격할 때도 있지만 서로 조화를 이루며 살아가니
어찌 보면 산다는 것이 기적이 아닌가 싶기도 하네요

누가 우리 부부 보고 천생연분이라 했던
나는 남편이네 하고 목에 꼿꼿하게 힘을 주고 있으면
아내는 나의 목에 핫팩을 대 주면서 말하지요
목이 풀려야 음식도 잘 먹고 건강해서 평생 해로 할 수 있
다네요

인생에서 가장 많은 시간을 함께 하면서 지내는 우리 부부
희로애락을 맛보며 생의 수레바퀴를 감사함으로 끌면서
빛과 소금이란 비전을 품고서 한 걸음 한 걸음씩 발을 옮기
지요
행복 품은 인생사를 글 속에 담아 두고 싶은 소망이 똑같
거든요

: 외손녀 딸

소우주에서 밖으로 나온 날
암흑에서 빛으로 바뀌었다
첫소리로 응애응애 하면서 말이다
아빠 엄마 사랑의 걸작품
신이 만들어 준 동산, 이든
기도 속에 너의 아빠 엄마는 기쁨의 눈물이 흐른다
한마디로 존귀하고 신기한 어린 생명체
아빠 엄마를 반씩 닮았나 보다
날마다 신의 사랑과 은혜로 건강하게 자랄 터
이 세상의 빛과 소금이 되어다오

ː 자화상

바람도 없는 모래 언덕에
무엇이 그리 두려워
허물어지는 모래성을
만들려고 하는가
군데군데 만들어 놓은
50년이라는 양철집 주변을
서성이다 보니 이미
은퇴할 나이가 되었다

아직까지 명주실 같은
연약한 목소리만 나올 뿐
대포알 같은 함성은 나오지 않고
바싹 마른 두 손바닥을
서로 비벼대며
분필을 들고 칠판에다
하염없이 흰 손수건을 그리며
흔들며 떠들어대고 있다

: 어느 시인의 고백

고뇌와 번민 속에서 시상(詩想)을 낚아
삼겹줄을 수십 번 엮어내고
해산의 고통을 이겨내면
마음에 밝은 미소가 태양처럼 다시 떠오른다

: 바라는 사회상(社會相)

거짓과 사기(詐欺)가 사라지고
정직과 진실이 확장되는 사회
부정과 부패가 없어지고
성실과 신뢰로 살아가는 사회로 살아갑시다

불평과 불만이 줄어들고
칭찬과 격려가 자리 잡는 사회
말보다는 행동과 실천이 앞서 가는 사회
바른말과 고운 말만 주고받는 사회로 살아갑시다

남의 눈 속에 있는 티를 빼게 하기 전에
자기 눈 속에 있는 들보를 빼는 사회
실망과 좌절보다는
용기와 비전으로 전진하는 사회로 살아갑시다

주는 것이 받는 것보다 복이 있는 사회
하루하루가 즐거움과 행복으로 이어지는 사회로 살아갑시다

: 영정사진

"살짝 웃고 편하게 저를 보세요!"
"자~. 찍습니다. 하나, 둘, 셋"
순간 눈앞에 번쩍 빛이 쏟아졌다
주름진 얼굴이 움찔하며 가슴이 굳어진다
처음 해보는 주연에 분 바른 얼굴에
자꾸 눈을 깜빡이게 된다
"눈을 깜빡이지 마세요. 아버님"
몇 번의 NG 끝에 무사히 촬영은 마쳤다

'벌써 세월이 이렇게 되었나'
사진관을 돌아서는 발길이 무겁나
언젠가 나의 사진이 생일 때 한 번씩
제사상에 올라올 것인데 곱게 차려입은 양복이
괜스레 무겁기만 하다
모처럼 모양내고 나온 나들이
산 위에는 낮달이 영정처럼 침침하게 걸려 있다

자아 인식에서 탐색하는 시간과 삶의 행로

김송배

(한국시인협회 심의위원, 한국문인협회 자문위원,

한국문인협회 부이사장)

자아 인식과 성찰의 의미

현대시의 정신은 그 시인의 정서와 사유(思惟)의 범주(範疇)가 어디에 머물고 있느냐에 따라 중심사상과 그곳에서 발현하는 주제가 어떤 지향점으로 의식의 흐름을 흡인하고 있느냐를 살피는 것이 대단히 중요하다.

이는 한 시인이 시적인 발상이나 동기가 어떻게 상황을 설정하면서 전개되고 있는지의 출발점이 바로 그 작품의 진가(眞價)를 이해하는 데 많은 공감을 제공하기도 한다. 이는 시인이나 독자가 서로 상관물에 대한 이미지의 투영이 융합하거나 화해하는 시법(詩法)이 발흥(發興)되었음을 의미한다.

대체로 현대시의 흐름이나 전개 양상은 자신의 존재를 인식하는 절차를 지나게 된다. 이는 자아의 인식은 곧 그 시인의 존재적 의미에서 탐색하는 인생이나 삶의 지향점을 모색하는 하나의 가치관의 정립이라고 할 수 있다.

여기 이병호 시인이 상재하는 첫 시집 『론 사이프러스』의 원고를 읽으면서 이러한 전제(前提)를 먼저 상기한다. 이는 이병호 시인이 의식하거나 인식하는 심저(心底)에는 그가 한생을 살아온 인생의 행로(行路)가 과거의 시간성에서 회상하면서 현재를 인식하는 단계를 밟게 된다. 그가 그 행로에서 탐색하는 주안점은 성찰의 의미적인 요소를 시적으로 해법을 찾고 있다는 점을 간과(看過)하지 못한다.

일찍이 영국의 시인 리처드는 우리의 일상생활은 정서 생활과 시의 소재 사이에는 차이가 없다고 했다. 이러한 생활의 언어적 표현은 시의 기교를 사용하게 되어 있다는 점만 근본적인 차이일 뿐이라는 말과 같이 우리 주변에서 사소하게 일어나는 일상적인 생활에서 추적하는 시의 소재가 바로 자아의 성찰을 탐색하는 한 방법의 시법일 것이다.

이병호 시인의 약력에서도 볼 수 있듯이 1978년에 도미하여 UCLA 교육학 박사과정을 수료하고 미국방 외국어대학에서 한국어과 교수를 35년 6개월간 봉직한 인생의 체험이 바로 자아를 인식하는 원류로 작용하고 있다.

우선 그는 '나 또한 위트가 없고, / 마냥 침묵을 지킬 자신도 없지만 / 아무렇지 않습니다. / 이유는 나름의 소신이 있기 때문입니다. / 세상은 재치 있는 사람을 선호한다지만 / 그렇지 못한 사람이 더 많습니다. // 대신 잘할 수 있는 나만의 특기가 있습니다. / 꼭 말해야 할 때 / 나는, 말할 수 있는 소신과 / 용기가 있으니 아무렇지 않습니다.(「용기와 소신」 중에서)'라는 어조(語調)와 같이 담담하면서도 세상과 삶을 통달(通達)한 자적(自適)의 사유가 성찰의 의미를 내포하고 있음을 알 수 있다.

바람도 없는 모래 언덕에
무엇이 그리 두려워
허물어지는 모래성을
만들려고 하는가
군데군데 만들어 놓은
50년이라는 양철집 주변을
서성이다 보니 이미
은퇴할 나이가 되었다

아직까지 명주실 같은
연약한 목소리만 나올 뿐
대포알 같은 함성은 나오지 않고
바싹 마른 두 손바닥을
서로 비벼대며
분필을 들고 칠판에다

하염없이 흰 손수건을 그리며
흔들며 떠들어대고 있다

— 「자화상」 전문

이병호 시인은 자신에 대한 직접적인 현상을 묘사함으로써
그가 현재까지의 인생과 삶을 회상하면서 정립시킨 '자화상'이
다. 그러나 '군데군데 만들어 놓은 / 50년이라는 양철집 주변을
/ 서성이다 보니 이미 / 은퇴할 나이가 되었다.'는 어조에서는
화자는 숙연해지며 시인 이병호의 속마음을 이해하게 된다.

다시 그는 '대포알 같은 함성은 나오지 않고'라는 언술과 '분
필을 들고 칠판에다 / 하염없이 흰 손수건을 그리며 / 흔들며
떠들어대고 있다.'는 진솔한 언어가 바로 그의 인생의 진실이며,
시적 흡인력이 된다. 어쩌면 초라하고 연약한 인생의 성찰하는
행로가 적나라(赤裸裸)하게 형상화하고 있는 것이리라.

김형석 교수는 그의 글 「내가 있다는 일에 관하여」에서 '내가
있다는 것, 이것이 모든 것의 출발이며 이로부터 세계와 우주
는 그 자리와 의의가 있게 된다. 우주의 중심이 나에게 있으며
세계의 모든 무게가 나라는 초점 위에 머물고 있다'는 논지와
같이 '나'라는 존재의 확인이 바로 우주와 세계의 중심이 거기
에서 생동감을 부여하고 있는 것이다.

이병호 시인은 이러한 시간 속에서 어느덧 '고희'를 맞게 된다. '고희(古稀)가 / 눈앞에 와 있다 // 오늘은 십이월 삼십일일 / 해마다 찾아오는 날이지만 / 오늘은 유난스레 눈물이 난다 // 머릿속에는 / 아직도 어릴 적 엄마의 얼굴이 / 스멀스멀 출렁이는 기억으로 / 향기로운 내음으로 펴져 있는데 // 늦은 귀갓길인데도 / 동네 몇 바퀴 몇 바퀴 돌아온 것밖에 없는데 / 코앞에 고희가 / 빙그레 웃고 있다. (「고희」 전문)'에서와 같이 인생은 서글프고 외롭고 고단한 삶의 행로를 빙빙 돌고 있는 고독감에 젖어 있다.

이병호 시인은 이러한 인생관을 정리하고 '그래도 행복은 찾는 웃음은 계속 찾아야 할 것 같습니다. / 어차피 한 번뿐인 인생인데 행복을 위해서는 이보다 / 못할 일이 어디에 있겠습니까. (「행복을 찾는 길」 중에서)'라거나 '행복은 풍요에 있는 것이 결코 아니다. / 모든 것에 감사한 마음을 가져야 행복해진다. / 불신보다는 조그만 일에도 감사한 마음을 느끼면 / 그게 행복인 것이다./ 행복해서 감사한 게 아니고 / 감사해서 행복한 것이 아닐까 싶다. (「행복」 중에서)'라는 행복론의 전환으로 그가 자존의 인식을 단정하면서 시적 진실을 정리하고 있다.

시간성과 동행하는 인생행로

이병호 시인은 시간성에 대하여 많은 집중을 하고 있다. 이 시간과 동행하는 인생행로가 다변적이다. 그 시간에 따라서 구

축되는 인생의 지향점이나 가치관의 탐구가 다양하게 변환하는
시적인 전개과정을 읽을 수 있게 한다.

이와 같은 시간성은 과거와 현재, 미래라는 명징(明澄)한 개념
으로 인생과 대입한다면 우리 인간이 간직한 오욕(五慾)과 칠정
(七情)에서 상관하는 정감적인 행로가 재생되어 인식하고 성찰
하거나 미래를 기원하는 인생관을 재창조하게 되는 계기를 맞
기도 한다.

우리의 칠정(喜怒哀樂 愛惡慾) 중에서 노(怒)와 애(哀) 그리고
애(愛)가 우리의 일생을 통해서 각인(刻印)되거나 불망(不忘)의
이미지로 창출되어 주제로 투영하는 시법을 자주 대하게 되는
데, 이병호 시인도 이러한 우리 인간의 고유한 정(情)을 배제하
지 않는다.

대체로 현대시를 해부해보면 자애(self love)라는 대명제를 항
시 유념하면서 어떤 인생을 영위할 것인가를 탐색하는 경우가
많은데, 이병호 시인은 애(愛)에 관한 실생활(real life)에서 획득
되는 시간(혹은 세월)과 융화하고 화해하는 해법을 현현하고 있
음을 알 수 있다.

달린다
속도제한을 염두에 두고
행선지를 향하여

앞차도 보고 뒤차도 보고 옆차도 보면서

인생도 달리고

마음도 달리고

시간도 달린다

가정과 직장과 사회를 그리며

과거도 달리고

현재도 달리고

미래도 달린다

하루하루가 고달파도

인내가 보약이 되도록

긴장과 스트레스를 풀면서

즐거운 마음으로 달린다

희망도 달리고

꿈도 달린다

행선지에 도착할 때까지

내일을 향하여

행복을 싣고서

— 「고속도로를 달리며」 전문

　여기에서 이병호 시인은 '인생도 달리고 / 마음도 달리고 / 시간도 달린다'는 어조에서 알 수 있듯이 시간과 동행하는 것은 인생뿐만 아니라 마음이 상당한 비중을 차지하고 있다. 또한, 그는 '과거도 달리고 / 현재도 달리고 / 미래도 달린다'는

그의 내면에는 그에게 부여된 모든 시간이 함께 희로애락을 동
승시키고 있다.

　이병호 시인의 이러한 궁극적인 진실의 목표는 바로 '행선지
에 도착할 때까지 / 내일을 향하여 / 행복을 신고서'라는 결론
에 도달하게 된다. 결국, 우리 인간들의 '희망'과 '꿈'은 내일의
행복이 최종 목표라는 단순하면서도 소박한 기원의 의지가 '고
속도로'를 통해서 형상화하고 있음을 이해하게 된다.

　그렇다. 우리가 살아가는 노정(路程)에는 인내가 있어야 하고
'긴장과 스트레스를 풀면서 / 즐거운 마음으로 달'려 가야 한
다. 작품 「은퇴」에서도 '시간은 화살처럼 너무 빨리 날아가는데
/ 괴로움도 어려움도 산들바람에 실어 보내고 / 새로운 제2의
인생을 설계해 본다'는 새로움의 인본주의적인 자의식(自意識)이
발현되어 그의 관념이미지가 돋보이고 있다.

　그 세월에 희로애락도 많았는데
　가르치는 즐거움 속에서 나도 모르게
　머리가 희끗희끗해졌나 보다

　양어깨에 건강과 소망을 메고 터벅터벅 걸으며
　걸어온 길 뒤돌아 보지 않고 앞을 향하여
　인내는 쓰지만, 그 열매는 단것처럼

그는 '은퇴' 후의 인생 설계에 대해서 그동안 감당해온 체험, 즉 외연(外延-희로애락)에서 추출해낸 내포(內包)의 중심에는 '걸어온 길 뒤돌아 보지 않고 앞을 향하여 / 인내는 쓰지만, 그 열매는 단것처럼'의 확고한 가치관의 모색이 승화하고 있음을 이해할 수 있다.

이렇게 그의 심경(心境)에서 파생된 시간의 향훈(鄕純)은 다음과 같이 다양하게 형상화하고 있다.

- 가는 시간에 못다 푼 꿈일랑 맡겨 버리고 / 찾아오는 손님들을 상냥한 미소로 반기는 너 (「론 사이프러스」 중에서)

- 시간은 간다 / 공간을 초월하여 / 시작도 없이 끝도 없이 / 어제를 뒤로하고 / 오늘도 가고 내일도 간다 (「시간」 중에서)

- 어느 오후 한나절 / 따스한 햇볕 아래 공원 벤치에 앉아 시간 가는 줄 모르고 / 바닷가를 바라보면서 장미꽃을 피워가는 젊은 남녀가 정겹습니다 (「정겨운 모습」 중에서)

- 시간의 바퀴는 돌아가는데 변함없는 생활 / 어느 사람도 탓할 수가 없나 보다 (「캐나다 기러기」 중에서)

- 새하얀 물보라에 꿈을 실으 / 시간 가는 줄 모르는 사이 / 바다는 내 마음을 아는가 (「몬트레이 바닷가에서」 중에서)

- '벌써 세월이 이렇게 되었나' / 사진관을 돌아서는 발길이 무겁다 (「영정사진」 중에서)

이병호 시인의 시간은 '가는 시간'에 대한 아쉬움을 통한 성찰의 내면을 적시(摘示)하고 있는데 대체로 '오늘도 후회 없는 하루'이며 '하루하루가 행복한 삶으로 잇대어지도록 / 가벼운 발걸음을 옮기'는 것이며 '목적지를 향하여 정답게 걸어가는' 것이다.

또한, 그는 '소망의 내일이 기다리는 것'을 음미하면서 시간과 동행하고 있다. 이러한 시적 시간은 '시간은 영혼의 생명'이라고 강조한 롱펠로의 말처럼 생명이 인간의 시간을 진실로 유로(流路)하고 있는 것이다. 이러한 시간성은 우리 시학에서 시제(時制)라고 하는데 한스 메이홉에 의하면 '문학이란 다양한 양상을 띠고 있는 체험적 시간, 즉 의식내용을 의미 관련으로 조직하여 예술화한 것'이라고 한다. 이는 문학에서의 시간문제가 작가나 시인의 체험 곧 의식 내용과 근본적인 관련을 맺고 있음을 시사(示唆)해 주고 있다.

이처럼 우리의 시들은 대체로 현재 시제를 사용하고 있다. 한 시인의 체험이 어떻게 작품 전체에서 작용하고 있느냐에 따라서 그 시간성은 작품의 창작이나 감상에서 그 효과가 크게 나타나기 때문이다.

'인고의 삶'과 생명의 현장

이병호 시인에게서 다시 읽을 수 있는 중요한 주제의 탐색은 '인고의 삶'을 통해서 추적하는 이미지의 산책이다. 그는 삶의 현장에서 체험(추억한)한 '거짓과 사기'와 '정직과 진실', '성실과 신뢰', '불평과 불만', '칭찬과 격려', '말보다는 행동', '실망과 좌절', '용기와 비전'(이상 「바라는 사회상」 중에서)이라는 심원(心願)으로 내면에 잠재한 다양한 이미지들이 분사(噴射)하는 현상을 엿볼 수 있게 한다.

천 년의 침묵은 비碑가 되는가
인고의 삶을 이고 온 역경의 역사
햇볕 따가운 열기에 합장하는가
새들은 주변을 돌아 줄기를 트고
삶의 보금자리를 찾는다

어느 누구도 건들지 말라고
가시로 방패 삼아
지나가는 세월에 그리움 안겨 보내고
매서운 비바람에도
굳건히 서 있는 너의 자태
고난도 역경도 하늘을 우러르며
깊은 뿌리를 생명선에 지탱한다

내일의 환한 미소를 위해
긴 호흡 하늘로 내뿜는다

— 「선인장 소묘」 전문

여기에서는 '선인장'이라는 한 사물이 '너'라는 인간으로 변한 수사학상 의인법의 전형으로 작품을 이미지화하고 있다. '인고의 삶을 이고 온 역경의 역사'와 '고난도 역경도 하늘을 우러러'는 현장은 바로 우리 인간들이 '삶의 보금자리를 찾는 것이나 '깊은 뿌리를 생명선에 지탱'하려는 애환이 그의 진실로 승화하고 있어서 우리들의 공감영역을 확대하고 있다.

이병호 시인은 '내일의 환한 미소를 위해 / 긴 호흡 하늘로 내뿜는다.'는 어조의 결론은 휴머니즘을 열망하는 순수 인간들의 순정적인 이미지가 '선인장'을 비유한 지적인 시법으로 잘 현현되고 있다.

그는 다시 '가난과 굶주림이 있는 곳에 / 구제가 있기를 / 전쟁과 테러가 있는 곳에 / 평화가 있기를 / 수고와 땀이 있는 곳에 / 기쁨과 행복이 있기를 바라며 살아갑니다. (「바라는 것들」중에서)'라거나 '괴로움과 어려움이 있어도 한숨 쉬지 말고 / 짜증 나고 화가 나도 그렇게 살으시구려 (「그렇게 살으시구려」 중에서)' 그리고 '한세상 살면서 미워도 서로 풀고 / 싫어도 밝은 미소로 살아가시구려(「오해」 중에서)'라는 어조와 같이 인고의 세월을 인내하고 성찰하면서 살아가는 삶의 시법을 제시하고 있다.

갈등과 혼란의 세상에서
길가에 서 있는 크고 작은 나무들은
가는 세월에 생명을 맡긴 채

사랑스러운 호흡을 즐긴다

오가는 사람마다 서로 인사로 반기며
가는 길과 목적지가 달라도 가야 할 길은
반드시 가야 한다
갈 길이 멀고 험해도
희망의 가슴으로 나그네의 길을
오늘도 쉼 없이 걷는다

— 「바닷가 오솔길 따라」 중에서

곤하고 지쳐도
세상의 명예 권위 세월 속에 묻어 두고
마음의 등불 되어 생명으로 이어지는 님의 뜻을 따라
빛이 인도하는 대로
이 길을 묵묵히 걸어가야 하네

— 「나그넷길」 중에서

보라! 삶의 현장에서 이병호 시인은 조망(眺望)하는 '인생길'
은 바로 '생명'에의 갈구(渴求)이다. 그에게 착안(着眼)된 삶의 중
심에는 언제나 생명력이 강렬하게 유동(流動)하는 신념이 내재
되어 있다. 그는 '갈등과 혼란의 세상에서' 체험하게 되는 '나그
네의 길'이지만, 그에게는 언제나 '마음의 등불 되어 생명으로
이어지는 님의 뜻을 따라' 걸어가야 하는 확고한 기독교의 신심

(信心)으로 실천하고 있는 것이다.

　일찍이 장자(莊子)가 말했다. 개개의 육체는 죽으면 없어지는
지 몰라도 인류의 생명은 영원한 것이다. 섶을 인간의 육체에
비유한다면 그것을 태우는 불은 생명이다. 섶이 타고 없어지는
것을 볼 수 있지만 불은 이 섶에서 저 섶으로 이어져서 영원히
타오르는 것이라는 생명의 영원성을 강조하고 있다.

　이병호 시인은 이 밖에도 '우리 인생 모두가 빈손으로 왔다
가 / 빈손으로 가는데 / 우주를 가슴에 품고 / 이 세상 것 뒤
로하고 / 푯대만 바라보고 한발 한발 걸으련다 (『별이 빛나는 밤
에』 중에서)'라거나 '지금도 늦지 않으니 / 인생의 멋과 맛을 선사
하며 / 석류알 같아 보이리라 (『석류』 중에서)' 그리고 '인생에서
가장 많은 시간을 함께 하면서 지내는 우리 부부 / 희로애락을
맛보며 생의 수레바퀴를 감사함으로 끌면서 / 빛과 소금이란
비전을 품고서 한 걸음 한 걸음씩 발을 옮기지요 / 행복 품은
인생사를 글 속에 담아 두고 싶은 소망이 똑같거든요 (『우리 부
부』 중에서)'라는 어조처럼 인생과 인생사 그리고 생명의 갈구 현
장은 새로운 각오와 여망과 기원이 동시에 그의 사유를 지배하
고 있다.

순수 서정의 향기-자연 동화

　이병호 시인은 순수 서정시인이다. 그는 인생관뿐만 아니라,

대 자연관의 경지도 대단한 오감(五感)으로 발현되고 있다. 시
학에서 사물이미지의 창출은 시인이 간직한 깊고 넓은 지적 관
념의 결정체에서 출발한다.

우리 인체의 오관(五官-眼耳鼻舌身)이 감지하는 이미지는 시인
의 체험이 재생되면서 생산적으로 바뀌는 지적인 상상력을 제
공해 주는데 시인들은 이를 잘 수용하고 감응(感應)하면서 작
품을 탄생시키는 마력을 가지고 있다.

이병호 시인도 이처럼 시각적인 어떤 자연의 현상에서 추출
하는 순정적인 어조의 서정성은 남다르게 표출하고 있다.

초록빛 물이 톡톡 튀는
뒷마당에 나간다
조그만 쌍잎 어린 분꽃은
어느새 함박꽃 누이 같은
예쁜 꽃을 흐드러지게 만들었다

호박잎 가지잎 부추잎 고춧잎
아내의 바구니에는
어릴 때 뒷마당의 향취가 흘러나오고
뺨에는 분홍빛을 머금은
분꽃이 되어 있다

긴 세월의 골짜기를
건너온 태평양 바람이
분꽃 가지를 흔들 때마다
어린 아내의 분 냄새 같은
향기가 가만가만 풀어놓는
뒷마당의 분꽃

― 「분꽃」 전문

　우선 이 '분꽃'에서 이병호 시인이 응시한 정경은 향토적인 전
원의 한 풍경을 상기하는 정감이 물씬 풍기고 있다. 그가 흡인
하려는 이미지의 재생은 '호박잎 가지잎 부추잎 고춧잎 / 아내
의 바구니'에서부터 '향취'로 그를 자극한다.

　이러한 자연 서정은 현대의 문명생활에서 필연적으로 생성한
자연의 재발견이다. 누군가가 시는 자연의 모방이며 자연의 형
상이라고 정의를 내린 적도 있었다. 이와 같이 '긴 세월의 골짜
기를 / 건너온 태평양 바람이 / 분꽃 가지를 흔들 때마다 / 어
린 아내의 분 냄새 같은 / 향기가 가만가만 풀어놓는' 향수의
개념까지 변환하고 있다.

　봄이 오면
　깊은 잠에서 깨어 세상에 새 얼굴을 내밀고
　여름이 오면

보이지 않는 호흡으로 생명을 나누어주면서
파릇파릇한 삶을 즐긴다
가을이 오면
형형색색으로 즐거움을 선사하다가
어느덧 바람결에 지상에 낙하하면
색이 바랜 잎사귀 밟는 소리에 세월을 깬다
겨울이 오면
소리도 없이 벌거숭이 되어
세상사를 경험하다가
또다시 긴 잠을 청한다

— 「낙엽」 전문

이 '낙엽'에서도 이병호 시인이 천착(穿鑿)하는 시간 개념과 생명이 동일하게 작용하는 사계(四季)의 정경으로 형상화하고 있다. 어쩌면 우리 인간의 일생을 형상화한 주제가 자연의 개념으로 메타포어를 현현하고 있다.

이렇게 자연의 인격화에는 감상적 오류(誤謬)라는 비정적(非情的) 타자성(他者性)을 원용(援用)하고 있는데 동화(同化)와 투사(投射)라는 두 원리가 함께 작용하게 된다. 고 김준오 교수의 『詩論』에 따르면 동화(assimilation)는 시인이 모든 자연을 자신 속으로 끌어와서 그것을 내적 인격화하는 원리이며 투사(project)는 시인이란 정체가 없기에 그가 계속해서 어떤 다른 존재를 채우는 것 곧 자연 속에 자신을 상상적으로 투여하는 원리로 해석하고 있다.

이병호 시인은 이러한 개념의 정립으로 만유(萬有)의 자연과 대좌(對坐)한다. 그는 '오랜 침묵 속에 변함없는 고아한 자태 / 한 점 부끄럼 없이 화려함을 자랑하고 / 탐욕과 혼란의 세상에서 / 기다림을 먹고사는 꽃(「난」중에서)'이라는 어조와 같이 서정시(lyric)의 본래 목적인 그의 개인적인 정서나 경험을 노래하고 있다.

다시 그는 '스치는 바람결에 아름다운 미소가 넘친다 / 설레는 마음으로 넌지시 다가가니 / 말없이 뿜어내는 상긋한 향기 속에 / 사랑의 속삭임이 메아리친다(「뒤뜰에 핀 장미」 중에서)'라거나 '지금도 늦지 않으니 / 인생의 멋과 맛을 선사하며 / 석류알 같아 보이리라(「석류」 중에서)' 그리고 '눈비와 바람이 맵찬 / 추운 겨울 다 잊고 / 너끈히 한세상 이룬 / 꽃잔디밭 속을 거닐다 보면 / 아픔도 환한 빛이 되리라(「꽃잔디 해변」 중에서)'라는 순수 서정의 향연이 메아리치고 있다.

이처럼 우리의 서정시는 신라의 향가나 조선시대의 시조가 훌륭한 서정시라고 할 수 있다. 그러나 현대의 서정시는 사회의 복잡화와 비합리성에 대한 시인의 각성, 시인의 자의식의 과학적인 분석 그리고 음유(吟遊) 시인의 문화에 대한 멸망 등에 의한 정서의 자연적인 흐름의 서정은 모습을 감추고 정서화된 비

평을 내포한 경향의 서정을 많이 대할 수 있게 한다.

　고뇌와 번민 속에서 시상(詩想)을 낚아
　삼겹줄을 수십 번 엮어내고
　해산의 고통을 이겨내면
　마음에 밝은 미소가 태양처럼 다시 떠오른다

　이병호 시인은 「어느 시인의 고백」 전문에서 '고백'한 것과 같이 '마음에 밝은 미소가 태양처럼 다시 떠오르게' 하기 위해서 오늘도 '고뇌와 번민 속'을 헤매면서 '해산의 고통을 이겨내'는 정서적인 활동을 지속하고 있다.

　일찍이 하이데거가 말했다. 시는 우리들이 익숙해서 믿어버리고 있고 손쉽게 가깝고 명백한 현실에 비해서 무엇인가 비현실적인 꿈 같은 느낌을 일으킨다고 한다. 그러나 사실은 시인이 말하고 시인이 그렇다고 긍정한 것 그것이야말로 현실이라고 '시의 정신'에서 강조하는 것이다.

　이병호 시인은 이 시집을 통해서 자아 인식과 성찰의 의미를 탐색하고 있으며, 이러한 인생행로를 시간성과 동시에 추적함으로써 삶과 생명의 동반이라는 진실을 재발견하는 시법을 강구하고 있다.

　그리고 마지막으로 자연관에 대한 서정적인 심성을 투영해서 인간과 자연의 공존이라는 등식을 명징하게 정립하는 시인 본래의 정감으로 현현하고 있는데, 그의 내면에 원류를 두고 있는 시적 진실을 깊게 확인할 수 있는 계기를 제공하고 있다. 첫 시집의 출간을 축하한다.

※ Poetry Book in Korean & English ※

론 사이프러스

Lone Cypress

Lee, Byungho (Brian. B. Lee)

지식공감 도서출판

 Introduction

When a customer comes to a barber shop, the barber sits the customer on a chair and asks him what kind of haircut he would like that day. As per the customer's request, the barber trims, cuts, and puts a final touch on his hair. Only when the customer is satisfied, the barber finally puts on a smile.

Just like the barber, when a poet has an idea for a poem, he or she draws up an outline, thinks about the idea, and finally writes down the thoughts in his or her head. And if the poem does not satisfy the poet, a rewrite would surely follow until a satisfactory piece, after a period of perseverance, is completed. Only then the poet would put on a smile.

As someone who enjoys literature, I started writing bit by bit with a sense of duty and courage, and finally a small collection of poems has come to fruition. Not only for poets, I think all who consider themselves people of literature should consider their readers and have the responsibility or the obligation to write what the readers want or what will be read by people.

There is an old Korean proverb that says "A tiger dies and leaves his coat. A man dies and leaves his name." People who write should live harmoniously with nature and the society as their friends, and they should shed light on and embrace the emerging social aspects, values, and the views of life. Through literature they should also take the lead in purifying the sentiments of the society.

With my first published collection of poems, I shall use this opportunity and apply myself to writing more poems that are not only good by themselves, but are also read by many people.

I would like to express my deepest gratitude to Mr. Gilbert Kang, the president of the Korean Writers' Association, USA, who has been a tremendous help in writing and publishing this book.

> - May 2015. Byung-Ho Lee
> From Monterey, CA

contents

Part 3 Lone Cypress

Part 4 A Husband and a Wife

Part 1

Sea of flowers

⋮ The analogue age

The barber shop in my hometown village
The owner, looking at the empty shop
Flaps the fly swatter against the wall

The heat wave of August,
She fans herself with a fan that has holes
But the beads of sweat have formed on her forehead

Regardless, with a hope that is the size of a watermelon
While affectionately waiting for customers
She plays with a fan and a fly swatter
On a hot summer day

The shop used to be full of customers.
It has lasted the test of time with a pair of scissors
By cutting a customer's hair
And by trimming his bushy grey concerns away

Passing by the side door, next to the cracked mirror
There is a well full of jujube leaves
Making soap bubbles and rubbing the razors in the air
Thin freshly sharpened blades are laid down

Hanging on the wall of the barber shop
The cuckoo of the wall clock, singing a cuckoo's song
Goes backs to its home after agitating the
Stillness, stagnant inside a soap container

In this new age that worships quickness
Analogue seems slow and inconvenient
Missing the closeness from the old age
I write this poem on this sweltering day in August

⋮ Heartwarming Sights

In one afternoon, for half a day
Sitting on a bench under the warm sun, being unware of
the passage of time
It is heartwarming to see the sight of a young couple
enjoying the ocean and growing a rose flower together

An old couple in silence
Plodding along a path near their house, holding hands
It is heartwarming to see the sight of their unresolved time

Immersed in various autumn colors, breathing in the gentle
breeze
Stepping on the dead leaves and walking arm in arm
It is heartwarming to see a middle-aged couple walking up
to a mountain temple, leaving all the worldly things behind
them

In the early morning, with their packs on their backs
For a dream with friends and bright smiles all heading to
their school
It is heartwarming to see the sight of our school kids

In a rainy day, holding an umbrella together
Walking happily towards their destination
It is heartwarming to see the sight of smiles of young lovers

⋮ A flock of sparrows

Sitting on the branches
A flock of sparrows chatters away in my backyard

Yesterday
Today
And tomorrow
Percussion, wind, and
String ensemble are loud

When the flock of sparrows sings
I listen to it
And sing along with them
As a form of reciprocation
But they become startled and fly away in a hurry

I would like to share
With many people
With all animals
But feeling foreign
We become isolated, not understanding one another

: May

With the brimful sunshine
I stand on the sand dune
And unlock the latch
Of the closed mind of mine

Like the rising tide
The warmth of a spring breeze
Feels beautiful
Like azaleas in my hometown

The longing that spurts like water
Makes me want to rush out to
My friend' s house, who has a buzz cut
I wonder what everyone is doing now

This feeling of nausea for no particular reason
And my adolescence, which disappeared
A long time ago
The month of May in my hometown
Already lost its way
Came inside my heart,
Swelling a surge of waves

⋮ Balsam flower

On the day of my wedding
I colored my wife' s fingernails
With a balsam flower

On our first night
I colored my wife' s toenails
With a balsam flower

In our house in the United Sates
I carefully planted its seeds in my front yard
To color my children' s finger and toenails
With a balsam flower

Wishing to huddle around
And to talk about our old stories
While coloring us in a balsam flower
Where has everyone gone?
I am making vain efforts

: Chewing on an apple

One red apple
I chew on with my molars
The sweet sour juice
Crosses over my throat
No matter how wide my chest is
It does not want to be held

A fiery passion
Has it ever existed?
Time has passed, weakening my teeth
Only the chewing morals hurt

I put down the apple on my desk
Then on my computer
A logo of a bitten-off apple
Along with a leaf
Having been worried sick
All burned to black
Crashes into a bucket

: Sea of flowers(at Lovers Point Park)

Haedong
When you feel gloomy
Let's go visit the Lovers Point Park

At the beach
As if a pink color paint has been dissolved in it
To the field of flowers where even a shade can be dazzling
Let's hurry and go see the flowers

Through the unforgiving snow and rain,
Forgetting the harsh winter, and
Creating a world of wonders
When we walk through the field of flowers
Sorrow will become a beautiful light

Haedong,
When you feel gloomy
Let's go to the park and see the field of flowers
Where the spring sky and the powder pink color will greet us

⋮ The Sketch of a Cactus

Does the silence of a thousand years become a monument
A history of adversity enduring the life of long suffering
Are they praying with their hands towards the sky in this
burning heat
The birds fly around them, bringing the stems
To make their nest of life

Fending off all things
Using thorns as your shields
Passing along the longing to the passage of time
Even in a fierce rainstorm
What a poise to stand on the ground
Raising your heads up, whether in hardship or adversities
Guarding its lifeline with deep roots

For tomorrow' s bright smile
They breathe out their long breath into the sky

⋮ Pomegranate

How long has it been since the flowers bloomed?
Breaking the peel, out into the world
Bright red kernels show their faces
Like the bosom of a virgin lady
They are about to pop at any moment

Looking at it closely, it is a work of the Creator
Harmony and balance surging in waves
They stay in place, closely and in arrangement
With similes on their faces
They must be waiting for the perfect time
Fresh in taste while being sweet and sour
They tempt the tip of my tongue
It is still not too late
Providing the sapidness and the taste of life
They sure look like the seeds of a pomegranate
Blessed are those who give rather than take

⋮ Humming bird

The smallest bird of all birds
Flies towards a flower with a lightning speed

Stops in the air in a stationary state, flapping its wings at a
high speed
Using its awl-shaped beak it consumes the honey in an
instant
And moves around from flower to flower
It must be tired, resting and taking a break on a branch
It must be lonely, calls for his half
Whether it rains or the wind blows
Always looking for flowers
Without being intoxicated with the scent of flowers
A bird purely living on sweet and sour honey
Such a small creature with a flying speed like an arrow
Searching for flowers, it travels without rest

⋮ A rose in my back yard

It feels like yesterday that a bud was born
Without much ado and following time
A bright red rose in my back yard has blossomed

Beautiful smiles overflow in the grazing breeze
As I approach with my heart fluttering
The rose emits its fresh scent without a word

Whispers of love echo
As a reunited couple after a long separation

⋮ Orchid

Undergoing all the hardships of life
In order to bear a cluster of buds
How long did it have to endure a period of suffering?

Experiencing disappointments and hollowness
Out of stillness with patience as its only weapon
It billows one day, as it realizes its dream

Spurting its innocence and beauty
Incubating the smile of Mona Lisa
It makes the heart of a virtuous woman flutter

The long silence and its never-changing classical figure
Boasting its brilliance without feeling shy
In this world of greed and confusion
A flower living on the virtue of patience

When its pedals fall off with no one looking
Filling the poor soul with love
It is waiting for a loved one to return

: Fallen leaves

When spring arrives,
They wake up from their deep sleep and show their new
faces to the world

When summer arrives,
They share life with their invisible breathing

When fall arrives,
They present joy in various colors
And wake up time with the sound of people stepping on
them

When winter arrives,
They become naked without a notice
Experiencing the world
Only to go back to a long sleep

Canadian Wild Goose

⋮ Time

Time goes by
Free from the restriction of space
Without the beginning and the end
Leaving yesterday
It goes by, even today and tomorrow

Time goes by
In silence and without a sound

Time goes by
Without being irritated or complaining

Time goes by
Without stopping or resting
As water flows from the valley to the river
And to the ocean

Time goes by
As we cannot stop it
And as we cannot hold onto it

Time goes by
Having experienced all things in this world
Overseeing the joys and sorrows of life

Time goes by
Without you realizing it
Without me realizing it
With no one noticing it

Time goes by
Now and forever

：Sex slaves for the Japanese forces

The heaven cried and the earth also cried
During the Pacific War, not knowing what may lie ahead of them
The day they were forced into becoming sex slaves at such
delicate ages,
They experienced the scars of the bodies and pains of the mind
that they can never erase

Do they not have parents and their own families, the Japanese
soldiers?
Do they not have a shred of guilty conscience?

The day the greatness and the dignity of humanity were
completely trampled
As the Japanese emperor announced its surrender to the Allied Forces
Apologize and repent to the people of Korea
I make a promise once more

No matter the cost, let us not become a weak nation again
Today, as the wheel of history keeps turning
What do you try to distort history?
Every day, let us develop our nation' s strength

For the future of our country
As the springs comes after a long winter
The sun always rises after a dark night

⋮ Courage and Conviction

Jean de La Bruyère once said
It would be such a shame
To not have a wit and not be able to speak cleverly
Be that as it may
And a misfortune to not have discernment
To be able to keep silent

I am not witty myself
And not confident that I can keep my silence
But I am fine with it
The reason is I have my own conviction.
This world may prefer those who are witty
But there are more of us who are not witty

Instead, I have a special talent of my own
When it is time to speak
I have my conviction and courage
To speak up, so I am more than fine with that

⋮ Finding a Way to Happiness

My daughter asked me one day
Why are you always angry? Is there something going on
with you?
I had always thought I maintained a happy face
So her questions came as a wake-up call
I now wonder whether I make a frown face even when I
laugh

So I have been practicing smiling, on a mirror in my school
The first few times were awkward
I would flatten out the wrinkles in my forehead with a
spoon
And practiced for many, many days showing a generous
smile
It must have worked, and now my smiles have become
more natural
But I had to spend many days practicing smiling

My wife asked me
Why are you smiling for no good reason?
Do I look that trivial?
I had been smiling every day with pleasure,
But her questions made me feel I was blindsided in the
back of my head with a stone

Strangely, people who I encounter these days,
Anything good these days? Any hardships these days?
I am now being asked these questions that are at the
opposite ends of the spectrum

Regardless, I shall try to look for smiles that find happiness
After all, each of us has only one life to live, and
Is there anything that we would not do to find happiness?

: Grace

It is giving without expecting in return
With no way to repay
It has no end
It remains in our memories
It is amazing
It transcends both time and space
It is something that is beautiful
It is higher than the sky and vaster than the ocean
It is an infinite love
Without regrets

⋮ Rain

The rain is falling
The river beds and the soil of the rice paddy have all
cracked like the back of a turtle
And have all been burned by the reigning sun
The precious rain is falling

It puts the word "drought" to shame
Worrying people to the brink
The heavens must have heard
The desperate cries of the people
The sweet rain is falling

As the rain makes the ground wet, all things on earth start
to smile
And sprout out

Rain, Rain, keep coming down without rest
Until we are completely relieved from this drought
Until the wrinkles disappear from the foreheads of the farmers

Keep streaming down
Bright smiles leave an aftertaste
Our minds already wish for a bumper year
The late rain is sparsely falling

: Happiness

On the streets everywhere, there is an abundance of food
In an alley of food, many different smells vibrate my nose
On TV and the computer, they show food 24-7
Would that be why? On radio and newspaper as well, they
seem to talking about food all the time
Everything seems to be overfull these days
I grew up enduring poverty
But I cannot say I am happier now with all this stuff

Happiness should not depend on richness
We can truly become happy when we are thankful for
everything
Instead of distrust, if we can feel thankful for the smallest
things,
That should be happiness
We should not be thankful because we are happy
Perhaps we should be happy because we are thankful

⋮ Driving on a Highway

I am driving
Keeping in mind the speed limit
Toward my destination
Being mindful of the cars in the front, rear, left, and right
My life is driving
So is my mind, and
So is time

Toward my family, my job, and our society
The past is driving
The present is driving
And the future is also driving

Though each day is a burden
Being patient is my medicine
Relaxing my body and my mind
I am driving in a happy state of mind

Hope is driving
My dream is driving
Until I get to my destination
Toward tomorrow
Carrying happiness

⋮ A cold windy day

Over a blue carpet
A dancing flock of seagulls is flying
A singing voice of the chorus by the sound of the waves
From the empty sea shore
Where everyone has already left
A chilly wind blows over

The passing wind that pounds the shoulders
The wandering wind that frantically tears up the soul
The wind that leaves scars of blood

Like a skein of yarn
The exploring chilly wind caused a trouble
Over the sand dune
It goes away alone, uncovering the rags
My skinny fists are crying, saying it is too cold
Casting a long shadow, they utter a caw

⦂ Beef Soup House in the Mountain

It is cold outside and the snow falls in large flakes
The soup house is busy and hot, filled with its customers
Roe deer soup on one table, hare soup on another table

Pheasant soup on the other table, all singing in chorus
We make a toast with a mug of beer and unburden
ourselves
A history of memory is being written tonight
One of us speaks up "Living is all the same,
So what am I supposed to do"
In the soup house, it is full of family affairs and life history
Though it is a tough life to live
I give myself to the shining star lights
I want to be a bird, flying away, transcending time
This year is slipping away with only a few days left
I shall take care of all my unresolved tasks before time
disappears
And I shall decorate tomorrow with new dreams

: Canadian Wild Goose

Flying over the mountains and rivers for thousands of
miles during the winter
The wild goose finally made it here
To find life in this weather that is not too cold or too hot all
through the year
Having promised to go back when they first flew here
together
They must have forgotten to miss their hometown for a few
years
And gotten used to the living conditions here
The wheel of time keeps turning, but it must be the comfort
of never changing life
Who could blame them for staying for such life?

Feeding on grass in a hayfield, all walking in pairs,
While others swim peacefully in a pond nearby
The goslings follow their mommy who walks totteringly
Each day is relaxing without worries or concerns

How special is that love for the couple
When anyone approaches them nearby
With the look that says how dare you to approach this place

The male goose, with his head held high, looking around and shouting warning messages
Keeping a close watch on everything that goes by
The female goose, without concerns for anything, munches on grass and takes a nap
Taking time off and relaxing, forgetting the passage of time

Not caring about the fate of tomorrow
Though the road ahead is long and hard,
Hoping that each day leads to a happy life
They take their light footsteps

⋮ A Journey

I step on the earth one step at a time
Through a narrow road and a wide road
Every day I turn the wheel of life

The winding road and the straight road
Although the end of the road cannot be seen,
With a faint hope
Overcoming life' s vicissitudes
I am walking the path I am supposed to take

Though a long and vile journey awaits
With peace and patience as my friends
I must be on my way

In the journey of life
There are uphill and downhill roads
When suffering and trouble rush towards me
The short and the long routes
I must take

When I become fatigued and exhausted
I shall bury worldly honor and authority in time
Following the wishes of my dear who is my life and a
candle in my mind
As the light guides me
I shall walk on my path in silence

⋮ Drawing a Farming Village

Using a cow to plow the field
For the children who are in the city
With a straw hat on
Who sweats profusely in two streams
I still like the farmer

With their bodies bent with the promise of a bumper year
Humming a cheerful tune following the guide line
Who are planting rice
I still like the country women and the village women

Finished farming and their hair covered with a towel
Holding a hoe heavily with their hands behind their back
Walking with a bit of stoop to make dinner
I still like the women who are heading home

Setting a basket on her head and carrying a snack
And a makgeolli kettle in one hand
She is walking along the ridges between rice paddies
I still like the woman

Hearing the order to drive away the birds
Putting up scarecrows
Carrying warm sunshine in its heart
I still like grazing time, carried on the wind

Ripening rice with its head bowed down
Embroidering the golden field
I still like their singing in the gentle breeze hoping for a
good harvest

Part 3

Lone Cypress

: Fireflies

Every night
The clubs of goblin
Dance in the forest

The egg ghost and the short ghost
Light up the ghost fires in their tails
In the forest, every night
They dance and dance
In the forest, throughout the night

The eyes are open yet mostly closed
They are closed yet somehow open
Drowned in the color of blood
Struggling
In the same place without progressing

My wife is crying
My mind is dried up
The long lost face of my son
Became a firefly
The crying sound of the bug in the grass
Makes us worry deeply

⋮ My birthplace

Mountains in front and back of my house
By the brook and the road near the bank
Glowing yellow clouds descend from the sky
And set up a mud hut
As if a swarm of butterflies are dancing
They gush out yellow incense in their purest form
All over the village
The wind of acacia flowers
Shakes their two arms, and
Stuffs my nose
In no time
Like a yellow radish
Soaks my clothes completely with the scent

⦂ A starry night

When the day changes to night
The night gate opens its door
Countless starlights pour down from the sky as if large
flakes of snow
Glazing over the Milky Way
Standing on one spot on this earth
We exchange silent greetings with our eyes
When I am lost and wander from place to place
I see the North Star, a journeyman's coordinates
In this silence and stillness
Suddenly a shooting star draws a line at a scary speed
For all of us, we come here empty-handed
And return empty-handed

Carrying and embracing the universe in my heart
Turning my back on the world
I shall take one step at a time towards the post
All things in this world
They are desires of passion and insights, or boasting of this life
If I can live proudly without feeling one ounce of shame
My mind is already is in heaven
In this starry night

⋮ Prayer

He visits me
For a conversation
He asks me
If I am faithful
He urges me to repent
For the paradise is near
Thank you
I love you
For being my light and salt
For you are the lamp under my feet and light for my path
I shall deliver the letter of gospel to the whole world

In Jesus' name

⋮ Along the Seashore in Monterey

The sky opens its gate and the ocean opens its mouth
Bright sunshine wears a smile on its face
A few scattered clouds get on board, carried by the wind

The mountains far away put up a folding screen under the sky
The seagulls carry hope flying towards their destination
As I indulge in this landscaping painting
The fishing boat in the harbor sings a song wishing for a
full load of fish
Memories from the past start to roll like a movie

When the calm waves become angry at the rocks
Unresolved torment becomes completely shattered
Carrying dreams in the spray of water
Without realizing the passage of time
Does the ocean understand me?
The wheels of life keep turning
The place where we buried our past in the sand
Awaits the hope of tomorrow

⋮ Seashore

The sea water
Makes the white bubbles, and
Throws them up temporarily in the air
Then, it rolls the pebbles
After playing with the water drops

Charrr, Dorrr,
Without needing company of others
It plays happily in solitary

A seagull dives into the ocean
And tosses the barnacle that it catches into the sky
When the barnacle comes back down and hits the rock
Smacking its lips
The seagull eats the barnacles sucking up all of its juice

Without concerns
For having been called a bird head
It continues to dive into the ocean
And carry the barnacle high up in the sky
And repeatedly drops them onto the rocks nearby
Over and over

⠆ A Rock near the Seashore

Clouds of mist at down
Pour down like a drizzly rain
The ocean without stopping
Mines white jewels

On the horizon far away
With my eyes carved out
Drunk by the fishy smell of the sea
That snuggles into my nose
Till the night stars become friends
While gazing at the horizon
It became my circumstance to be a protector of the island

⋮ Waves and rocks

Calm waves by the smiles of a gentle breeze

As if they were lightly dancing along

Are pulled in and pushed out

When the furious waves spurt anger onto the rocks

They never vent their rage, only to throw up white foam of patience

How have they endured such hardships of life?

Beaten, torn, scratched, and broken by the waves

They have spent their lives in silence for tens of thousands of years

Though their faces have changed from one shape to the other

Leaving all the hardships and pains behind

Sending all the selfish desires by the waves

As a ship sailing in the fair wind

They run carrying an armful of blue happiness

⋮ Along a path by the sea

Carrying the vestige of ancient times
On the side of a precipice on the Pacific
Along the coastline lays a path on which
People walk or run
Ride bicycles
The red sun with its ambition
Rises again as always
A few pieces of drifting clouds
Go on a voyage as sailboats

When the ocean swells against the rocks
Emitting their anger
A cloud of spray puts them to sleep
The fresh morning air
Touches the heart
And a beautiful smile flies over the blue sky

Mist rises from far away
The sea breeze without saying a word
Scrapes along my collar
The seagulls from early in the morning
Seeming looking hungry
Wanders around the blue sky exclaiming busily

In the world of conflict and confusion
The tall and small trees along the roadside
Trusting their lives to passing time
Enjoy their lovely breathing

The comers and goes welcome one another exchanging greetings
Though with different paths and destinations
They must go their ways
Though being a long and difficult way to go
A traveler's journey with a hopeful heart
I walk along the path without rest

⋮ Mountain

A rest area for cumulus clouds,
The mountain has stood there in silence for tens of thousands
of years
Whispering with the sun in the daytime and with the stars at night

Though it suffers from rainstorms and heavy snow
It always forgives with a simple smile

Disappointment and despair
Sublimated in a mother' s disposition
Hope and courage blaze up

It accepts challenges by men
Yet it tests the limits of men

Unchanged despite the passing of time
Whether I am nearby or far away
Befriending patience, you are always there
So I climb up on you

Inside the wheel of life
All things in this world are shaken up
Yet you are still and silent
Oh Mountain, please tell me something
Today as usual, I lift my eyes looking towards you

⠆ Lone Cypress

It must be your fate
To never stand on the ground
Overcoming the hardships of time
On top of a bluff, facing the Pacific Ocean
You standing alone putting down roots

Making friends with the sea breeze and the mist
Exhaling sonata
Awakened from a light sleep by the deep breaking waves
Leaving the unrealized dreams to the passing time
You always welcome your guests with a tender smile

Facing my reality
I utter a silent monologue
That this is how I live
Responding that happiness is nearby,
You wish to live today without regrets

Part 4

A Husband and a Wife

⠇ The field of words

Today as usual, I am wrestling with you

Clenching my fists,
Pounding on my chest,
Plucking my hair, and
Running to the field of words,
There is very little progress
And my hands already search for another cup of coffee

No matter how hard I try to win against you
I seem to be overmatched
To win this way
To fling you like I always imagined
I just end up with a cramp in my head

The high, blue sky and my old hometown
Keep visiting me in my memories
The homely old days of mine
Make me feel gloomy,
Blocking
The busy road
To the space in the future

But because of you, the field of words
With all different types of vegetables,
When they blossom and bear fruits
The tears in my eyes, and
The swamp of this moving feeling are so rewarding

Today
I head to my field of words, and
I shovel deep into the ground,
Water the field
And with the harvested fruits
I can feel like running forever……

⋮ Seventieth Birthday

My seventieth birthday
Presents itself right in front of my eyes

Today is December thirty first
This day comes every year
But today it brings tears to my eyes

In my head
The face of my mother from my youth
As memories rolling like waves
Spreads out all over my body in a fragrant smell

It is a late night going back home
And I have only circled around the town a few times
But right in front of my face
My seventieth birthday is smiling at me

⋮ Retirement

I taught at a university for 35 years
It was the time for me to hang up my hat
The stress and the tension accumulated from all those years
All seem to be melting away like snow

Time flies so fast, like an arrow leaving a bow
Sending away the past agonies and difficulties in the gentle
wind
I design a second chapter of my life

Through the years, I have experienced the joys and sorrows
of life
I must have enjoyed teaching greatly
For my hair have gone grey without letting me know

I walked along the path carrying health and hope on my
two shoulders
Towards the front and never looking back
Knowing patience is bitter but its fruit is sweeter

⋮ Misunderstanding

Misunderstandings are bound to happen
Is it because our views and ways of thinking are different?
Or is it because our capacity of understanding each other is
too small?

Misunderstandings are bound to happen
Is it because our times are different?
Or is it because our circumstances are different?

Misunderstandings are bound to last
Is it because the strength of our feelings is different?
Or because we do not understand each other's intentions?
We are to misunderstand each other
But in this one and only world, let's resolve all
misunderstandings
Without the hate and dislike and live with bright smiles

⠿ Money, what are you

Money, what are you?
Because of you, couples become married and divorced
Money, what are you?
A husband and a wife are separated and get remarried
Money, what are you?
You cause conflicts between parents and their children
Between brothers and sisters
Money, what are you?
Because of you, people live or die
Money, what are you?
You define a successful person from a failure
Money, what are you?

Because of you, we love and we hate
Money, what are you?
Because of you, an illness can be cured or left untreated
Money, what are you?
Because of you, we laugh or we cry
Money, what are you? Because of you, we live richly or
poorly
Love of money is the root of all evils
So earn adequately and live within your means

⋮ What I wish

I live wishing that there would be a dialogue
Where there is solitude and lonesomeness
That there would be an understanding
Where there is conflict and misapprehension
That there would be truth
Where there is falseness and distortion

I live wishing that there would be a reconciliation
Where there is aggression and dispute
That there would be a ray of hope
Where there is darkness and shadows

I live wishing that there would be forgiveness
Where there are mistakes and blunders
That there would be love
Where there is hatred and jealousy

I live wishing that there would be aid
Where there is poverty and hunger
That there would be peace
Where there are wars and terrorist acts
That there would be joy and happiness
Where there is trouble and sweat

⋮ You just live like that

Do not ask when and where you were born,
You just live like that despite your gripes and dissatisfaction

Do not draw a sigh despite your suffering and troubles
You just live like that when you are chafed at and angry

Do not be apprehensive though your future is unclear and
uncertain
You just live like that when you are worried and concerned

Don' t blame others and don' t meddle with others'   lives
You just live like that and be thankful with what you do

Do not compare your life with others
You just live like that, for life is beautiful if short

Do not give up on faith, hope and love
You just live like that and believe in God, who opens doors
for us

: A Husband and a Wife

We were born on this planet and we found each other as a
couple
We first met with the goal of a marriage, secretly glancing
at each other from top to bottom
Only after a few months, we rang a bell informing the
world of a new start
The forty years we spent as a married couple have flown
like an arrow

Becoming captives of the fluttering words "American
Dream"
There was a time we couldn' t even feel gravity after
stepping on this new land
Though we have had our share of disagreements, we have
lived harmoniously
And to a degree, living together for such long has been a
miracle

Some say we are a match made in heaven
Saying I am the husband in that heavenly couple and
holding my head up high
My wife puts a heat pack on my neck and tells me
Your neck must be relaxed so that you can eat well and stay
healthy for us to live together forever

We spent the majority of our lives staying together
Going through the joys and sorrows of life together,
As we thankfully pull the cartwheel of life
We move forward step by step, holding onto our vision of light and salt
Sharing the same wish of storing our lives of happiness in writing

： My daughter's daughter

The day when you crawled out of the microcosms
Darkness turned into light
Your first sound of crying as an infant
You are a masterpiece of love from your dad and mom
A garden that God had created for you, Eden
In prayer, your dad and mom sheds tears of joy
In a word, you are a noble and an amazing new life
Taking after your mom and dad equally
Every day you will grow healthy with God' s love and grace
Please be the light and salt of this world

: Self-portrait

On a sand dune free from wind
What was I so afraid of
And make a sand castle
That will collapse eventually
Wandering around
The house with a tin-roof
For over 50 years
Now it came a time to retire

Like a thread of silk
Only a feeble voice can be heard
A cannon ball like voice is no longer
My dried up palms
I rub them against each other, and
Draw a white handkerchief
Absent-mindedly on the board using a chalk
And make noise while waving it

⋮ A confession of a poet

Capturing the muse through torment and agony
Concocting three lines a few dozen times
Overcoming the pains of birth
A bright smile in my mind rises up again like the sun

: What I Wish for our Society

Let us live honestly and confidently, in a society where
Lies and fraud will disappear
Honesty and truth are welcomed
And unrighteousness and corruption can no longer exist

Let us live exchanging only righteous words, in a society
where
Complaints and grievances will go away
Compliments and encouragement are firmly established
And actions speak louder than words

Let us live marching toward courage and vision, to a
society where
Instead of being disappointed and discouraged
We can correct our own faults
Before we criticize those of others

A society where giving is more blessid than receiving
Let us all live in a society where every day is filled with joy
and happiness

┆ Photo of a Deceased

"Smile a little and look this way!"
"Alright~ I' ll be taking the picture. One, two, three"
A bright light flashed in my eyes
My wrinkly face flinches a little and my heart stops
As my first role as a lead character and with all this make up
I can' t help but blink my eyes
"Please do not blink your eyes, sir"
After a few NGs, the photo shot was complete

'I must have been unaware of the passing time'
As I return from the studio, my feet become heavy
At some point, a photo of mine will be used for my
birthdays
On a table for a memorial ceremony, so being dressed up in
a suit
Feels somewhat heavy for me
An outing in a long time, all dressed up
The moon in the middle of the day hangs above the
mountains like the portrait of a deceased person

Exploring time and life's
journey through self-awareness

Song—Bae Kim

Review Board Member, 〈Society of Korean Poets〉

Advisor, 〈Korean Writers Association〉

Vice Chairman, 〈Korean Writers Association〉

• The meaning of self—awareness and self—examination

To understand the spirit of modern poetry, depending on the poet' s emotion and the range of ideas, it becomes important to consider where the central thought of the poet and the manifestation of subjects stemming from it are directed as well as how such flow of consciousness are absorbed.

The starting point of how the poet sets up his or her poetic ideas and motives can provide us with sympathy in understanding the true value of the poet' s work. This implies that the prosody of a fusion or reconciliation has sprung up in projecting an image regarding the correlative of the poet and his/her reader.

Overall, the flow or the understanding of the development of modern poetry goes through the process of self-realization. This realization of self can be seen as establishing one's values in seeking a direction in one's life or exploring the meaning of one's existence.

We are constantly reminded of such premises as we read through the collection of Mr. Byung-Ho Lee's first poetical work 『Lone Cypress』. The course he took throughout his life takes its steps in realizing the present time by remembering the past. The emphasis that the poet seeks in his path cannot be overlooked - the point where he searches for solutions of the elemental sense in self-examination.

Richard Edwards, an English poet, once said our daily lives do not differentiate the emotional life and the material for a poem. As the only fundamental difference in the linguistic expression from that of our daily lives is from the technique of poetry, searching for material for poems from our mundane daily lives is one way for self-examination.

As we can see in his profile, the poet, Mr. Byung-Ho Lee, immigrated to the United States in 1978, and finished a doctoral course in education from UCLA. Since then he served as a tenured professor at the Defense Language Institute Foreign Language Center in Monterey, CA, for over 35 years. This experience becomes the root of understanding the poet.

First, 'I am not witty myself, / And not confident that I can keep my silence // But I am fine with it / The reason is I have my own conviction / This world may prefer those who are witty / But there are more of us who are not witty // Instead, I have a special talent of my own / When it is time to speak / I have my conviction and courage / To speak up, so I am more than fine with that. (From 「Courage and Conviction」).' As we can see in his tone in, we can see his self-examination connotes calm, yet self-content, grounds that are well versed in life.

On a sand dune free from wind
What was I so afraid of
And make a sand castle
That will collapse eventually
Wandering around
The house with a tin−roof

For over 50 years

Now it came a time to retire

Like a thread of silk

Only a feeble voice can be heard

And a cannon ball like voice is no longer

My dried up palms

I rub them against each other

And draw a white handkerchief

Absent—mindedly on the board using a chalk

And make noise while waving it

— 「Self—portrait」

As for the poet, Mr. Byung-Ho, Lee, describing the truthful
state of his inner self becomes a 'self-portrait,' erected by his
life in retrospect. However, in the following tone 'Wandering
around / The house with a tin-roof / For over 50 years / Now
it came a time to retire,' we see the narrator becomes solemn,
and we can finally understand the inside of the poet.

Then, 'A cannon ball like voice is no longer' and such
honest language in 'Draw a white handkerchief / Absent-
mindedly on the board using a chalk / And make noise
while waving it' represents the truth of his life as well as

his poetic charisma. To some degree, searching for the path in his humble and delicate life is plainly embodied in his work.

In his work 「Regarding My Existence」 written by Professor Kim, Hyung-Suk, he asserts that 'The fact that I exist is the starting point of everything, and through this, this world and the universe have their places and purposes. The center of the universe resides in me, and all the weight of the world is also focused on me.' Like this statement, identifying one's 'self' allows the center of the universe to assign the liveliness of life.

The poet, Mr. Byung-Ho Lee, now comes to face his 'Seventieth birthday.' As in 'My seventieth birthday / Presents itself right in front of my eyes / Today is December 31st / This day comes every year / But today it brings tears to my eyes // In my head / The face of my mother from my youth / As memories rolling like waves/ Spreads out all over my body in a fragrant smell // It is a late night going back home / And I have only circled around the town a few times / But right in front of my face / My seventieth birthday is smiling at me (「Seventieth Birthday」)' his life is immersed in a sense of loneliness as he is isolated and circling around life's harsh paths.

Though he identifies his view of life in this way, 'Regardless, I shall try to look for smiles that find happiness / After all, each of us has only one life to live, and / Is there anything that we would not do to find happiness? (From 「Finding a Way to Happiness」)' or 'Happiness should not depend on richness/ We can truly become happy when we are thankful for everything / Instead of distrust, if we can feel thankful for the smallest things, / That should be happiness / We should not be thankful because we are happy / Perhaps we should be happy because we are thankful (From 「Happiness」)' he concludes his self-awareness and identifies his poetic truths by turning to eudemonics.

• The path of life that accompanies time

The poet, Mr. Byung-Ho Lee, focuses on time throughout his work. His paths in life that accompany time seem multilateral. We can read his directing point of life that is established according to time or the poetic process of development in which his search for values takes different directions.

If the nature of time substitutes, in lucidity, one's past, present, and the future, then our affectionate paths based on the five desires and seven passions become reproduced, and it becomes an opportunity to recreate one's view of life that examines self or that wishes a future.

Among the seven passions, anger, sorrow, and love are the ones that we most often we face in our daily lives and are therefore projected as the frequent subjects in poetry as never forgotten images. The poet, Mr. Byung-Ho Lee, does not exclude these inherent human elements of affection in his work.

In most cases, when we analyze contemporary poetry, most poets explore which paths to take in life, while being mindful of the main proposition of self-love. Regarding love, the poet, Mr. Byung-Ho Lee, incarnates the solution to bring reconciliation and rapprochement of time, realized in his everyday life.

I am driving
Keeping in mind the speed limit
Toward my destination
Being mindful of the cars in the front, rear, left, and right
My life is driving
So is my mind, and
So is time
Toward my family, my job, and our society

The past is driving

The present is driving

And the future is also driving

Though each day is a burden

Being patient is my medicine

Relaxing my body and the mind

I am driving in a happy state of mind

Hope is driving

My dream is driving

Until I get to my destination

Toward tomorrow

Carrying happiness

— 「Driving on a Highway」

As we can see in his tone in 'My life is driving / So is my mind, and / So is time' what accompanies time is not only his life, but his mind as well. In addition, in his inner self, which can be seen in 'The past is driving / The present is driving / And the future is also driving,' his remaining time rides together with all human feelings.

Thus, the poet's ultimate goal of truth is 'Until I get to my destination / Toward tomorrow / Carrying happiness' and arrives at the aforementioned conclusion. After all, we understand the poet's simple and plain wish of a final goal of 'hope' and 'dream' for our humanity is tomorrow's happiness. This volition is embodied through a 'highway.'

In our journey through life, we should be patient and have the mindset that 'Relaxing my body and my mind / I am driving in a happy state of mind.' In his work 「Retirement」, he confesses that 'Time flies so fast, like an arrow leaving a bow/ Sending away the past agonies and difficulties in the gentle wind / I design a second chapter of my life,' and his sense of identity based on humanism is realized here, and his idealistic sense shines through the said poem.

Through the years, I have experienced the joys and sorrows of life
I must have enjoyed teaching greatly
For my hair have gone grey without letting me know

I walked along the path carrying health and hope on my two shoulders
Towards the front and never looking back
Knowing patience is bitter but its fruit is sweeter

Regarding his plan for life after 'Retirement', his experience he has managed throughout his life, that is, at the center of his self, extracted from the joys and sorrows of life is 'Towards the front and never looking back / Knowing patience is bitter but its fruit is sweeter' and we can see that his seeking of implacable values has sublimated.

This way, the scent of time derived from his heart is embodied in various ways as can be seen in the following.

- Leaving the unrealized dreams to the passing time / You always welcome your guests with a tender smile (From 「Lone Cypress」)

- Time goes by / Free from the restriction of space / Without the beginning and the end / Leaving yesterday / It goes by, even today and tomorrow. (From 「Time」)

- In one afternoon, for half a day / Sitting on a bench under the warm sun, being unaware of the passage of time / It is heartwarming to see the sight of a young couple enjoying the ocean and growing a rose flower together (From 「Heartwarming Sights」)

- The wheel of time keeps turning, but it must be the comfort of never changing life / Who could blame them for staying for such life? (From 「Canadian Wild Goose」)

- Carrying dreams in the spray of water/ Without realizing the passage of time / Does the ocean understand me? (From 「Along the Seashore in Montreal」)

— 'I must have been unaware of the passing time' / As I return from the studio, my feet become heavy. (From 「Photo of a Deceased」)

The poet shows his inner side of introspection through the inconvenience of 'passing time', and mostly it is about 'each day without regrets' and 'hoping that each day leads to a happy life / They take their light footsteps' while 'Walking towards one's destination.'

Moreover, he accompanies time while appreciating 'hope awaits for tomorrow'. This poetic time is the passage of human time channeled through by life, as Henry Wadsworth Longfellow said of 'time as the life of soul.' This time in poetry is referred to as the 'tense', and according to Hans 'Literature is an experimental time with different aspects. That is, contents of awareness are organized according to sentimental relevance as an art form.' This implies time in literature is fundamentally related to the writer or the poet's experience, that is, the writer's contents of awareness.

Therefore, poems utilize the present tense in most cases. Depending on how a poet's experiences affect his or her entire work, time has little effect on creating or appreciating art.

• 'Life of suffering' and the stage of life

What we observe from the subjects is that the poet, Mr. Byung-Ho Lee, uses the strolling of an image through a life of suffering. What he has experienced throughout his life such as 'lies and fraud', 'honesty and truth', 'complaints and grievances', 'compliments and encouragement', 'actions rather than words', 'disappointment and discourage', and 'courage and vision' (From 「What I wish for our society」), and these images stored in his inner side are sprayed out.

Does the silence of a thousand years become a monument?
A history of adversity enduring the life of long suffering
Are they praying with their hands towards the sky in this burning heat?
The birds fly around them, bringing the stems
To make their nest of life.

Fending off all things
Using thorns as your shields
Passing along the longing to the passage of time
Even in a fierce rainstorm
What a poise to stand on the ground
Raising your heads up, whether in hardship or adversities
Guarding its lifeline with deep roots

For tomorrow's bright smile

They breathe out their long breath into the sky

— 「The Sketch of a Cactus」

Here, the object of 'cactus' becomes a human called 'you,' a rhetorical personification being used for an image of the poem. 'A history of adversity enduring the life of long suffering' and the following phenomenon 'Raising your heads up, whether in hardship or adversities' represents that the joys and sorrows of his life sublimate into truth and enlarge our capacity for sympathy.

The poet concludes from the following tone that 'For tomorrow's bright smile / They breathe out their long breath into the sky.' And such pure image of pure people who desire for humanism is expressed as a 'cactus' in an intellectual prosody.

Again, the poet states that 'I live wishing that there would be aid / Where there is poverty and hunger / That there would be peace / Where there are wars and terrorist acts / That there would be joy and happiness / Where there is trouble and sweat (From 「What I wish」) or 'Do not draw a sigh despite your suffering and troubles / You just live like that

182

when you are chafed at and angry (From 「You just live like that」)'   and   'But in this one and only world, let's resolve all misunderstandings / Without the hate and dislike and live with bright smiles (From 「Misunderstanding」).'   In these tones, he patiently endures and self-examines the suffering of life, and suggests a poetic way to live a life.

In the world of conflict and confusion
The tall and small trees along the roadside
Trusting their lives to passing time
Enjoy their lovely breathing

The comers and goes welcome one another exchanging greetings
Though with different paths and destinations
They must go their ways
A traveler's journey with a hopeful heart
I walk along the path without rest

— From 「Along a path by the sea」

When I become fatigued and exhausted
I shall bury worldly honor and authority in time
Following the wishes of my dear who is my life and a candle in my mind

As the light guides me
I shall walk on my path in silence.

— From 「A Journey」

Look! On the stage of life, what the poet, Mr. Byung-Ho Lee, glimpses for the 'path of his life' is thirst for 'life.' At the conceived center in his life is the faith in life that flows intensely. He experiences a 'journey' 'in the world of conflict and confusion', but he walks 'following the wishes of my dear who is his life and a candle in his mind' fulfilling a sound Christian faith.

A long time ago, a philosopher called 'Jang-Ja' said the following. When we die, our bodies may disappear, but the life of humanity is forever. If brushwood were the body of a human, the fire that burns it would be life. He emphasized such eternity of life with an analogy that the wood may burn out and disappear, but the fire will move from one brushwood to another, maintaining itself forever.

Furthermore, we see in the following tone 'For all of us, we come here empty-handed / And return empty-handed / Carrying and embracing the universe in my heart / Turning my back on the world / I shall take one step at a time towards the post (From 「A starry night」)' or 'It is still not too late / Providing the sapidness and the taste of life/ They sure look like the seeds of a pomegranate/ Blessed are those who give rather than take (From 「Pomegranate」)' and 'We spent the majority of our lives staying together / Going through the joys and sorrows of life together / As we thankfully pull the cartwheel of life / We move forward step by step, holding onto our vision of light and salt / Sharing the same wish of storing our lives of happiness in writing (From 「A Husband and a Wife」), that a new determination, expectation, and his wish all simultaneously dominate his reasoning on the stage of life.

• The scent of pure lyric − Assimilation with Nature

The poet, Mr. Byung-Ho Lee, is a lyric poet in the purest sense. Not only his view on life, but also on nature, are expressed through his five senses. In poetry, an image of an object is created from the fruit of a poet's deep and wide intellectual conception.

The images that our five senses feel are portrayed through the experiences of the poet and provide us with intellectual imaginations. Poets have magical powers to create art through accepting and sensing these images.

Mr. Lee expresses differently when it comes to his lyricism using his simplistic tone extracted by certain visual and natural phenomena.

I step outside to my backyard
Where the green water sputters
What used to be a tiny flower with two leaves
Has grown to be a splendidly beautiful four o'clock flower
Just like its sister, magnolia

Pumpkin leaves, eggplant leaves, leek leaves, chili leaves
From my wife's basket
Flow out the savor of the backyard from my youth
Its cheek wearing pink color
Became a four o'clock flower

The wind from the Pacific Ocean
Flown over the valleys of the long years
Shakes up the branches of the four o'clock flowers
Oh, the gently released scent
Of the four o'clock flowers in my backyard

— From 「The Four o'clock Flower」

First of all, in his poem 'The Four o' clock Flower' , the scene the poet has glazed over exudes the scenery of indigenous countryside. The recollection of the images he wanted to absorb was 'pumpkin leaves, eggplant leaves, leek leaves, chili leaves / from his wife' s basket' that simulate him with their 'savors.'

Such lyrical nature is the rediscovery of nature, created inevitably from the civilized life of the present era. Some say poetry is defined by the imitation as well as the imagery of nature. As this, 'The wind from the Pacific Ocean / Flown over the valleys of the long years / Shakes up the branches of the four o' clock flowers / Oh, the gently released scent' changes even the concept of nostalgia.

When spring arrives
They wake up from their deep sleep and show their new faces to the world
When summer arrives
They share life with their invisible breathing.
When fall arrives
They present joy in various colors
And wake up time with the sound of people stepping on them.
When winter arrives
They become naked without a notice

Experiencing the world

— 「Fallen Leaves」

The work 'Fallen leaves' embodies the notion of time
that the poet searches for as well as the scenery of the
four seasons in which the concept of time and life apply
equally. In some sense, these topics which embody the lives
of humans are realized through the concept of nature as
metaphoric expressions.

In this way, personification of nature borrows cruel
and different sentimental mistakes, and two principles of
assimilation and projection act together. The late professor,
Juno Kim, wrote in 'The theory of poetry' that assimilation
is the principle of personification of all things in nature,
and projection is when a poet continuously projects him/
herself into nature using imagination, for the poet's identity
does not exist in poetry.

The poet establishes these ideas and sits face to face with
all things in nature. He describes 'The long silence and its
never-changing classical figure / Boasting its brilliance
without feeling shy / In this world of greed and confusion /
A flower living on the virtue of patience (From 「Orchid」)'. In
this tone, the poet sings personal emotions and experiences
which is the original purpose of lyric poetry.

Again, as we can see from ＇Beautiful smiles overflow in the grazing breeze / As I approach with my heart fluttering / The rose emits its fresh scent without a word / Whispers of love echo (From「A rose in my back yard」)＇ or ＇It is still not too late / Providing the sapidness and the taste of life / They sure look like the seeds of a pomegranate / Blessed are those who give rather than take (From「Pomegranate」)＇ and ＇Through the unforgiving snow and rain / Forgetting the harsh winter / Creating a world of wonders / When we walk through the field of flowers / Sorrow will become a beautiful light (From「Sea of flowers」)＇ lyrical feast echoes throughout his work.

In this way, our folk songs from the period of Silla or sijos from the Joseon period are considered excellent lyric poetry. However, recent contemporary lyric poetry shows tendency to predicate emotional criticism due to the complicated nature of our current social situations, the poet＇s awakening to irrationality, the poet＇s scientific analysis of one＇s sense of identity, and one＇s desire of the culture of a wandering poet. The old-fashioned lyric where emotions flow freely has mostly disappeared.

Capturing the muse through torment and agony
Concocting three lines a few dozen times

Overcoming the pains of birth

A bright smile in my mind rises up again like the sun

The poet, as he 'confessed' in 「A confession of a poet」, for 'A bright smile in his mind to rise up again like the sun' he 'captures the muse through torment and agony' and continuously perform such emotional activities 'overcoming the pains of birth'.

Heidegger says the following. Poetry enables us to feel like we are in a non-realistic dream, compared to our reality that is familiar, close, and easy to believe. In actuality, 'The Spirit of Poetry' emphasizes that what poets say and agree to is our reality.

With this collection of poems, Mr. Byung-Ho Lee explores the meaning of self-awareness and self-examination. And by simultaneously following his journey through life in relation to time, he seeks rediscovery of a truth that life and living must accompany one another.

Lastly, by projecting his lyrical mind toward his outlook on nature, the poet expresses using his own warmth and establishes an equation of humans coexisting with nature. This collection provides us with a chance to identify with his poetic truths rooted deep in his mind. I congratulate him on his first collection of poems.

강양욱 번역
kangyx@hotmail.com

WA University bachelor's
UCI University Master
UCI University Doctor of Philosophy

매실과 눈깔사탕 (Mesil and Eyeball Candy)
콩만큼 점수 받은 날 (A reward in the size of a peanut)
정담의 향기 (The Fragrance of a Warm Conversation)
시 한 송이 피워 (Growing a flower of poetry)
론 사이프러스 (Lone Cypress)

Lone Cypress
론 사이프러스

초판 1쇄	2015년 08월 15일
지은이	이병호
발행인	김재홍
디자인	박상아, 이슬기, 박선경
마케팅	이연실
발행처	도서출판 지식공감
등록번호	제396-2012-000018호
주소	경기도 고양시 일산동구 견달산로225번길 112
전화	310-382-664
팩스	02-322-3089
홈페이지	www. kwaus.org
가격	10,000원
ISBN	979-11-5622-111-1 03810
CIP제어번호	CIP2015022459

이 도서의 국립중앙도서관 출판시 도서목록(CIP)은 e-CIP 홈페이지
(http://www.nl.go.kr/ecip)에서 이용하실 수 있습니다.